THE LAST MILE

THE LAST MILE

A novel by
Blair Richmond

Book three of *The Lithia Trilogy*

Also by Blair Richmond,
books one and two of
The Lithia Trilogy:

Out of Breath
The Ghost Runner

The Last Mile

A novel by Blair Richmond

Book three of *The Lithia Trilogy*

Published by Ashland Creek Press

Ashland, Oregon

www.ashlandcreekpress.com

ISBN 978-1-61822-026-4

Library of Congress Control Number: 2014936985

This is a work of fiction. All characters and scenarios appearing in this work are fictitious. Any resemblance to real persons, living or dead, is purely coincidental.

Printed in the United States of America on acid-free paper. All paper products used to create this book are Sustainable Forestry Initiative (SFI) Certified Sourcing.

"These violent delights have violent ends
And in their triumph die, like fire and powder,
Which as they kiss consume."

— William Shakespeare, *Romeo and Juliet*

Part One: Serpentine

One

Ashes to ashes.

These words run through my head as I walk through the forest holding a man's wristwatch. A golden timepiece warped and charred by flames into some misshapen, glittering ingot. The time has been frozen at the exact moment its owner was consumed by the conflagration—nine thirty-five.

This was my father's wristwatch. Now it is all that's left of him—all but the memories. And these memories I also carry, though these are much heavier and much harder to bear—most of them are better left forgotten.

Still, by now even the most painful memories are slightly less painful—my dad and I had a rare chance to reconnect before he died, an opportunity I know I should feel grateful for. Our last days and weeks together were not exactly warm and fuzzy, but during what turned out to be his very last moments, he seemed to have turned a corner, becoming a father I might've liked to know.

Yet if he'd lived he may have changed back again; he always

did—nice one moment, vindictive and sneaky the next. It's probably better that everything related to my father is now and forever in the past.

I've spent most of my life feeling alone, and certainly since I ran away, to Lithia, I've been on my own. But until now I haven't been an orphan—the last member of my family to walk this earth. My mother has for years lain buried in the town cemetery, and now I'm saying good-bye to my father here on this mountain.

There has to be a reason for it all—the death of my mother, then my father, both so violent and premature. There has to be a reason they both died in these hills, high above Lithia, the town of my birth, the town I now call home. But what is the reason? It's not easy finding one. Maybe it's just bad luck. Or maybe it is meant to be, and I'll never know why.

Ashes to ashes.

Ashes are all around me, everywhere I step, over charred branches and tree trunks, burnt leaves and grasses. The smell of charcoal wafts up as I step lightly on the blackened earth.

Ashes are all around, and yet I have none to spread. There wasn't much left of my father when they found him—only the watch. He'd been up here looking for me, thinking I was trapped by the wildfire as it blew down the hills toward Lithia. But I had already escaped the fire; I'd found my way down by a different route. I was safe, worrying about him at the same time he was running into the fire looking for me.

It was the first truly selfless act I could remember from my father. He'd put on quite a show in the weeks before that, telling me he wanted us to be a family again, telling me he wanted to help me save the land I'd inherited here—only to turn around and steal it from me. He didn't care about me, or the land, or the animals who make their homes here—he only cared about money. It was his only persistent goal in life: to get rich.

My father spent his life in constant pursuit of a quick buck, and even as he scammed people he didn't realize that he was vulnerable to the same scams himself. He used the developer Ed Jacobs to take the Horton property from me—and then he was shocked when Ed Jacobs turned around and used my father to take the land for himself.

Despite the flames that tore through here, ravaging the beginnings of Ed Jacobs's development, most of the trees remain healthy and untouched. Fire is nature's way of housecleaning, clearing the undergrowth of all the dead matter so that new life can grow. Fire tells the older trees to release their seeds, which they do, and, in turn, they give birth to the next generation of forest. In nature, fire is a necessary evil.

My father never understood that the land is a gift; he was always seeking something from it, only interested in what he could take from it. Since I was a child, he'd been looking for gold in these hills, and he never found it. Ironically, I was the one who finally found the gold my dad knew existed here—I'd found enough to buy the land back, and enough to care for it and keep it undeveloped, free of humans forever.

I am more like my mother—she loved this land, which is why Mrs. Horton had willed it to her, and that's how it eventually ended up coming to me. My mother died on the trails when I was just twelve. Back then, everyone thought it was a bear attack—and most still do. I know better.

This part of the forest is now famous for mysterious, fatal "bear" attacks of the worst kind—and yet no bear is ever seen or heard around the time of these incidents. The authorities simply blame bears because they don't know who to blame, and the locals have taken to just pretending it can't happen to them or hoping it never will. After my mother died, the killing stopped for a long time—but lately, it has been happening all too often.

After my mom died, I was dragged by my drunk father to Texas, where I got by until I couldn't take it anymore. I finally ran away, back to Lithia, the only place I knew to go, the only place where I remembered having good memories. After I returned, I began to find the life I always dreamed of living. It hasn't been easy—I've lost friends, I've lost love, I've lost my father—but I do know that I'm back where I'm meant to be.

And I've also learned that everything comes full circle. My mother raised me to treasure the land, and because of her friendship with an old widow who loved her, the land will now be protected. My father entering the circle again, my mother's ghost making an appearance—it all spun and spun, the land won and lost and won again—and now, here I am, full circle, wandering in search of the secret pond that my mom and dad had brought me to as a child to swim, the pond in which I later discovered the lost entrance to the gold mine.

I keep hoping I'll see my mother's ghost again, even though I know I won't. She had a role to play—to make sure I became the caretaker of the Horton land. And, thanks to her, I did, though the journey nearly cost me and Roman our lives. And now that her job is over, I won't be seeing her again.

But she's still with me. I touch the necklace around my neck—a polished stone of serpentine held in place by a silver chain—the one thing my father gave me that I'll treasure forever. My mother's necklace.

I'm still wandering, and I'm no closer to finding that pond.

The landscape has been so transformed that there are no familiar landmarks to go by—and I wouldn't be surprised to learn that the pond, and the mine within, is lost forever.

I'll have to make do with the land in front of me.

I set down my backpack. I open it and take out a small camp shovel and get to work digging a small hole.

I had hoped to find the spot where I'd discovered the gold not so much to say good-bye to my father but to seal it up for good. But I imagine the earthquake that rumbled through here did the work for me. The land always takes care of itself.

Once the hole I've dug appears deep enough, I hold my dad's watch over it. I had taken gold from the earth so I could save the earth. That's what I tell myself. And now it's time to return gold to the earth—and to put my father to rest.

"Good-bye, Dad," I say, and then I drop the watch into the ground.

I feel as though there's more I should say, but I can't think of what it might be. In the end, we didn't know each other well. I stand for a moment, staring down at the watch, thinking of his last moments, of the day he gave me my mother's necklace. It's the one thing he never took back, probably because it has no monetary value, only sentimental value. But the fact that he wanted me to have it means the world to me.

I like to think that he is in a better place now, happy at last, free of material obsessions. I wonder if he is with my mother, whether they have reconciled or have become whoever they once were together. Wherever they are has to be easier and less complicated than being here, in the real world.

I fill in the hole with dirt and ashes and stomp it solid, until it blends in with the rest of the ground. That's when I realize that

I've done such a good job of concealing my work that, unless I put up something to mark this location, I won't be able to find my way back.

But maybe it's better this way. The memories will never be lost, and the rest is just a watch frozen in time, returned to the earth. It's better if I forget. Say good-bye forever.

"Rest in peace," I say.

"Amen."

The voice comes from behind me and nearly stops my heart. I spin around.

It's Victor. His face is pale, his eyes glowing red, and he is standing way too close for comfort.

I'm not unused to vampires—after all, I've fallen in love with two of them. But they are different from Victor. Roman and Alex have both given up blood, while Victor is as hungry as ever. Right now, his fangs dangle over his lower lips.

"What are you doing here, Victor?"

"Paying my respects."

"This doesn't concern you," I say.

"Well, my dear Katherine, the truth is, *you* concern me," he says. "And if you don't mind my saying, I should likewise concern you a great deal. Didn't Roman or Alex warn you about walking in the woods alone?"

"I'm not afraid of you."

"Ah, but you should be."

He's right. I should be afraid. Any mortal should be afraid of this monster, this indiscriminate killer of men and women alike.

Yet I feel an almost serene calmness in my arms and legs. There is no longer any urge to run or even back away. I should be terrified right now, lungs frozen, ears pounding with the blood

I know Victor so desperately craves. My mind knows I should be afraid, and yet my body refuses to play along. And I begin to wonder if this is how death feels the moment before it becomes real. I don't want to die, but I also don't want to run any longer. Not from my past, not from myself, and certainly not from Victor.

He takes a step closer. At this point he and I could reach out and touch hands, not that I'm tempted to. I should take a step backward, and yet I don't. In fact, I feel the urge to step toward him, to force him onto his heels.

"Why don't you leave Lithia?" I ask him, stunned by my boldness. "You're not wanted here. You know that."

"Katherine, my sweet, why should I be the one to leave? I was here first, after all. It is I who should be asking you to leave."

I stand as tall as I can, though I can't possibly match Victor's stature. Still, my voice doesn't waver: "You'll have to kill me first."

"I fully expect to," he says. "I should have done away with you a long time ago. But I thought Roman would tire of you first and save me the trouble. I overestimated him. I expected him to remain loyal to his patron. To his destiny. To his nature."

"His nature has evolved. For the better. And if you weren't so stubborn, you'd follow his lead. Roman and Alex no longer need to kill people, and they've never been happier."

"They're freaks. Freaks of nature."

"No, Victor. You're the freak. You're an anachronism."

He smiles. "Anachronism? I'm a vampire. I'm an anachronism by design."

"That's where you're wrong. Everything evolves, or at least has the potential. Everything and everyone. It's how we survive. And you and your kind will never survive unless you evolve.

You'll have to change."

"Is that right?" His eyes narrow and his voice grows deep, like the bone-rattling roar of a lion. "Were these the same words you used to brainwash Roman?"

"I didn't brainwash him. He changed his mind entirely on his own."

"You inspired him, surely. You led him to the proverbial river."

"I merely told him that he could live a life free of guilt. That's what inspired him. Knowing he didn't have to spend the rest of eternity preying on others and leaving behind a wake of suffering. Are you telling me you have no guilty conscience? No guilt whatsoever?"

"If one has no conscience, then one has no need for guilt."

Victor's fangs are growing longer, his eyes burning red. I know I should back up, turn, run—anything to protect myself from this beast. Yet I'm not moving—or I can't move; I'm not entirely sure. It's as if my body is no longer under my command; I'm frozen to this spot.

He takes another step, and I feel the chill of his breath.

I remain still.

"Guilt," he says, with a low, hideous chuckle. "What a romantic and utterly useless concept."

"People who say they feel no guilt," I tell him, "are those who feel the most remorse." My voice sounds strong and certain, though I am all too aware of how much closer he's getting—and how few options I have.

"Then why don't we test that theory with you, my Katherine?" He seems to rise above me, and I have to look up to keep his face in my sights. "Let's see how much—or how *little*—remorse I feel once you are no longer among the living."

Then his hand is on my shoulder, in a death grip, and the air around me freezes icy cold—and all I can see is Victor's face, closer and closer, his mouth open wide, fangs dripping, and I close my eyes, ready to die. The words still ringing in my ears.

Ashes to ashes.

Two

A bright flash of lightning knocks me backward into a tree. I hear the sound of an otherworldly scream, smell sulfur in my nostrils, and open my eyes to see Victor on the ground in front of me, a hand over his face.

Smoke drifts up from his mouth. He rises unsteadily to his feet, sizing me up.

I don't know what just happened. I look up at the sky, but it's clear and blue—not a cloud anywhere. Where had the lightning come from?

Victor is staring at my neck, fangless, his eyes dark and angry. "Your necklace," he says. "Where did you get it?"

"It was my mother's." Instinctively I reach up to my neck. It feels warm to the touch, as if it has just emerged from an oven or microwave. I remember my mother used to think it brought her good luck. Of course, she was not wearing it the day she died.

Now I'm wondering: Could it be more than good luck? Could the necklace be so powerful that it had just saved my life?

Victor holds out his hand. "Let me have a look."

I step backward. "I don't think so." I run my hands along the smooth edges of the marbled green stone.

"You are fortunate to have had such a generous mother. Pity she wasn't wearing it the day Alex found her on the trail."

My anger fueled, I take a step toward Victor, and, amazingly, he takes a step back.

"This isn't over between us, my dear," he says. "As a matter of fact, it is only just beginning."

He turns and becomes a blur of movement as he disappears into the woods. The next thing I hear is the sound of my lungs exhaling. I begin to pace, with one shaking hand on my necklace, as if to protect it, as it had somehow protected me. I don't know what exactly happened, but whatever it was, I just faced death head-on and survived.

"Katherine."

I spin around, my heart leaping into my throat, ready for another attack.

But it's not Victor—it's Roman, running up the trail. He's not wearing running clothes, just jeans and a T-shirt, so it's clear that he's not out on a jog. That he's coming for me.

"What are you doing up here?" I ask. I still wonder how he instinctually seems to know when I need him. He and Alex both have this same uncanny ability.

"I had quite a disconcerting sense that you might be here," Roman says. "I also feared that Victor was not very far away."

"Is he ever?" I say.

Roman embraces me, and I collapse into his strong arms. Then I remember my necklace and how it hurt Victor. I push Roman away.

14

He looks surprised and hurt. "What is the matter?"

"My necklace. I don't want to hurt you."

"Your necklace?" Confusion quickly turns to recognition. "Katherine, did Victor attack you?"

"He tried to. But my necklace—it fended him off. I think it burned him somehow. He wouldn't come near me after that."

Roman has a knowing look, but he doesn't say anything.

"It's like I have garlic around my neck," I say, prodding him to tell me something.

"That's a myth, Katherine. Some vampires actually have quite a fondness for garlic." There is teasing in his voice—rare for my ever-serious Roman.

But right now I want answers, not jokes.

"Roman." I give him a look. "Are you going to tell me what's going on with this necklace, or do I have to guess?"

"I don't want this to give you a false sense of security," he says. "Yes, your necklace protected you. This time. But Victor is persistent and creative. He will find a way around it."

"I don't understand. If it can ward off Victor, how come it doesn't hurt you?"

"Because I'm no longer a killer," Roman says. "Make no mistake—I'm well aware of its power. But because I have changed, because I have no desire to harm you, it cannot harm me."

I pull the necklace, still warm, away from my neck to get a better look. "What's the deal with this stone, exactly? My mom thought it was good luck, but I figured she was just being superstitious."

"The stone is serpentine," Roman says. "And serpentine is a very old stone. Not just any type of rock but one blessed by the Native American spirits. The natives believed that serpentine held special powers, that it could channel energy from the earth. What you're wearing is an ancient necklace."

"My dad said she got it from someone in her family."

"Remember, Mrs. Horton was a pioneer descendant, and she was like family to your mother."

"So you think my mother got this from Mrs. Horton?"

"It's possible."

"She was trying to protect her," I say with a sigh. "And it didn't work."

"Mrs. Horton was a wise lady," Roman says. "And I know for a fact that Victor always hated Mrs. Horton. He was very careful to avoid her."

"That's why she lived such a long life." I sigh again. "I guess it's an accomplishment in this town to die of old age."

Roman nods. "Victor has lorded over this region for a very long time—there have been absences, thankfully, but he always returns. Perhaps the natives figured out a way to protect themselves from him. And perhaps some pioneer families learned a trick or two as well."

I run my fingers over the stone. I wish I knew why my mother wasn't wearing it that fateful afternoon on the trail. I'll probably never know, though I suspect my father might've taken it from her, thinking he might pawn it. She was always "losing" things— a pair of earrings, a tennis racquet—and she didn't learn until later that he would pawn whatever he could that might be worth something, anything to make a quick dollar. Maybe he couldn't get any good offers for what looks like an ordinary stone held with a thin, inexpensive chain of silver. It is beautiful to me, handmade with love—but I can understand a pawn shop owner not seeing much value in it. No gold, no gems.

Yet what a valuable stone it is.

I suddenly feel so much more powerful knowing that I can stand up to Victor, knowing I can live my life without worrying about what's lurking behind the trees and outside my cottage door. Maybe I can finally get a full night's rest for once.

"I told you that you shouldn't be up here alone," Roman says.

"I wanted to say good-bye to my father."

"It's not safe."

"I'm not going to live in fear. You'd be proud of me, Roman. I didn't back down to that monster. Not a step."

But he doesn't look proud; his pale, handsome face is taut with worry. "Katherine, please, I need you to listen to me very carefully," he says. "That necklace does not give you immunity. Victor may not be able to touch you while you are wearing it, but that doesn't mean he will stop trying to hurt you. He will stop at nothing."

"What does it matter, as long as I wear it all the time?"

"He will try to take it from you, directly or indirectly. Promise me you won't come up here alone."

It's been more than a month since I've been able to go running with any sort of consistency, with the craziness of school and theater, but I've longed to start again. I know if I just nod and smile, this will ease Roman's worries—and yet I can't do it. I can't bring myself to lie to Roman, and I'm too stubborn to let a man— or a vampire, for that matter—tell me where I can or can't go.

"I'm sorry, Roman. I can't promise you that."

He gives me such a disappointed look that I almost change my mind. Almost.

"Roman, I'm sorry," I say. "But you know that's no way for me to live, always looking over my shoulder, or staying close to you like some child in need of protection. And you said yourself that Victor isn't going to leave me alone no matter what I do."

"True. But that doesn't mean you should be alone so often. It's too risky. You must let me protect you."

"But you can't protect everyone in this town. The best thing you can do is figure out a way to get Victor to leave Lithia once and for all. That's the only way we'll all be safe."

"Believe me, Katherine, I've tried. But how do you bribe someone who has no interest in money?"

"So what does he want, exactly?"

Roman says nothing, and then I realize I already know.

"Okay, I guess it's obvious—he wants me dead. But why?"

"You know why."

I guess I do. "Because you love me."

The look on Roman's face tells me I'm right. "He knows you're my only true weakness, Katherine."

Then comes the sound of leaves rustling in the forest around us, and both of us go on alert. I feel my body tensing, ready for Victor to reappear—though I should know by now that when there is noise, I have much less to fear, since Victor makes no sound at all.

Still, we can't know what's coming around the bend, and I hold my breath until I realize that it's moving faster than a bear; it might be a deer. Then, from around the bend, moving swiftly, comes a woman dressed in form-fitting running gear and dark sunglasses. She blows right by, stepping nimbly to the edge of the trail to get past us and not breathing heavily at all. She looks familiar, though I can't place her; she went by too quickly for me to say hello even if I could remember who she was.

I feel the urge to join her; it's been weeks since I've run this trail. I'm a little envious and decide right then that it's time I got back into fighting shape. With Victor breathing down my neck, I'm going to need to be.

I turn back to Roman. "Is that hidden pond around here?" I ask. "I couldn't seem to find it."

He nods. "Why do you ask?"

"I want to see it again. Can you take me there?"

"Will you stop running by yourself if I do?"

"No."

He shakes his head. "I had to ask."

He brushes past me to lead the way, and I follow a few steps behind as he holds the branches for me. We are off the trail now, climbing through thick forest and deep ruts in the earth.

After a few minutes we arrive at the pond. We're in the middle of the woods—I'd never have found it again on my own.

I stare down at the water, at this magical place. It's where my mother and father used to take me when I was a child, where I swam and played and dove down deep. It's where I discovered the gold and, thanks to that discovery, saved Lithia—and all these trees and all the animals that need them—from Ed Jacobs.

I reach down to touch the icy water and am met with a different sensation entirely. "Ouch!" I pull back, stung by the heat.

I look up at Roman in shock, but he doesn't seem surprised.

"Why's it so hot?"

"Mount Lithia," Roman says.

"What do you mean?"

"The earthquake that sealed the gold mine shut must have set free geothermal channels," he says. "So now it appears we have a hot spring."

"Just like that?"

"Just like that." But I can tell there's something he's not telling me.

"Out with it," I say.

"I beg your pardon?"

"Tell me the truth, Roman. Hot springs don't just happen like this. Do they?"

"It's unusual," he admits.

"Is Mount Lithia in danger of erupting?" I ask.

"It's a volcano," he says. "That is what volcanoes do."

"I know that, but are *we* in danger?"

"I don't know."

"That's comforting."

"You shouldn't worry. If this mountain gets close to exploding, I'll let you know."

Suddenly a woman's scream pierces the forest.

Before I can turn my head toward the sound, Roman has disappeared, a blur woven into the thick trees.

Vampires move far too quickly for most humans, and though I may be a competitive runner, I'm out of shape, and it's hard for me to keep up. I do my best, following the noise. Still, I make a few wrong turns, and when I finally reach the trail, I turn right, hoping I'm heading in the right direction.

I round the bend, and there is Roman, helping a woman to her feet.

It's the runner—the woman who passed us earlier. She looks badly shaken up, and she has several bleeding scratches on her arms and neck.

And then I remember her. Her name is Erica Summers; she's a professional runner and, the last time I checked, she hates my guts. She was the reigning champion of the women's Cloudline competition, and I narrowly beat her in the last race—a grueling run to the top of Mount Lithia. She couldn't even look me in the eyes after that race, and I didn't think she'd ever forgive me for beating her.

She meets my gaze but doesn't appear to recognize me. She must *really* be shaken up.

"I don't know what happened," she says, her voice trembling as much as her body. "Somebody grabbed me from behind. And then"—she wrinkles her brow—"I don't know, I sort of blacked out or something. Next thing I knew, here you were. You must've scared him off."

Roman holds her steady. "It was a bear."

She looks startled, then doubtful. "It couldn't have been a bear. It happened too fast, and I didn't hear a thing. No way a bear can move that fast."

Apparently Roman doesn't remember what a know-it-all Erica is, or he'd have come up with a more convincing story.

"I saw him," Roman says, his usual serious expression and old-fashioned way of speaking adding a bit of credibility to his words.

"Really?" Erica spins her head around, as if to glimpse the bear for herself. "Are you *sure?*"

"I'm quite positive," Roman says smoothly. "A black bear, a male juvenile. When he saw me, he turned and ran away."

Erica is still looking around for evidence. "I'm pretty sure I'd have heard something as big as a bear."

"They don't always announce their presence," Roman says.

"And you were in the zone," I say, speaking runner talk in hopes of changing the subject. "I don't hear anything myself when I've got a runner's high on."

Erica looks Roman right in the eye. "What did you say to it?"

He puts on a surprised look. "What did I say—to the bear?"

"I could have sworn I heard you shouting."

"I'm afraid you're mistaken," he says with a patient smile. "You've had quite a fright."

Erica stares at him for another long minute. Then she sighs and begins brushing the dirt off her legs.

"Strange," she says.

"Bears usually don't hurt people," I offer. "You must've startled him or something."

She's still ignoring me, talking directly to Roman. "You know what else is strange? It got really cold, just before I got attacked, like I was having a flash of hypothermia. That's never happened to me before."

If there had been any doubt in my mind—which there hadn't—this tells me that it was definitely Victor. I catch Roman's eye, and he quickly looks away.

"That sounds unusual indeed," Roman says. "Let us walk you back to town. It sounds as though you might need to see a doctor. You may be getting ill."

"And we'll alert the authorities about the bear so they can put up warning signs," I add. I feel as though it's our best shot at keeping people away from Victor, but on the other hand, bear warnings aren't likely to deter the residents of Lithia from going up into the hills. They'll be a little more heads up, maybe, but it won't stop them. They all know that bears are generally harmless and prefer to steer clear of humans.

Erica finally turns to me, and I see the recognition in her eyes. "I know you. From the race."

I nod.

"Pat, right?"

"Kat."

"You running Cloudline this year?"

"No," Roman says.

"Yes," I say, at the same time.

"Well, are you or aren't you?" Erica says.

"Actually," I admit, "I'm undecided."

"You injured?"

"No." I don't want to tell her I've let myself get out of shape.

"Then you've got no excuse," Erica says with a smirk. "What is it—afraid you won't be able to defend your title?"

"Not at all."

"If I'm running, bear scratches and all, you better be running."

More fun than saying yes to her challenge is answering with a little shrug, which seems to annoy her greatly.

Roman gives me a look and starts leading her down the path.

"Let's go back to town," he says. "I must be off to the theater soon."

Erica looks back at Roman and then, amazingly, she smiles— a real smile, something I thought this woman was incapable of doing. "Oh, you're that actor. You were in *Hamlet*, right?"

"He *was* Hamlet," I say, in a rather obnoxious and possessive way.

Roman smiles. Apparently even after more than a hundred years, he still enjoys having two females competing over him. I roll my eyes and follow them as Erica tells him about all the plays she has seen him in on her journeys up here to Lithia; she's flirting with him as best she can. I resist the urge to butt in, or to take Roman's hand in mine to show that he and I are together.

I distract myself by thinking about Cloudline. The race is just a few weeks away. With all the recent craziness in my life— losing the Horton property, getting it back again, my father's death, the fires—I had nearly stopped running altogether. Even though I knew the race was fast approaching, I've been telling myself that there will be other years, other races.

But I'm beginning to realize, now more than ever, that timing is everything. Just moments ago, Roman saved Erica by a matter of seconds, or less. They say you should live your life as if you only have a short time to live—that if you do, you spend time on all the things that matter. And the fact is, with Victor on a mission to get rid of me for good, I may only have a short time to live—for real.

What if this really is my last chance to run Cloudline?

Better to spend my time doing what I love most, whether or not Victor manages to get his way. The one thing that is true is that time does not favor the undecided. I have to be decisive and proactive.

And I want to run Cloudline.

I want to feel the rush of competition and the meditative runner's high that feeds me while I train in these hills. I want to challenge Erica again, to prove I can and will defend my title. Roman may not like my running up here alone, but he will have to understand. Or he can simply join me; Roman is an avid runner himself and winner of the last Cloudline race in the men's division; there could certainly be worse people to train with.

But what about Victor and his most recent violent streak, targeting innocents as he did with Erica? As we head back to town, my mind is still trying to figure out exactly what happened a few minutes ago. If Victor wanted to kill Erica, he would have done so. It would've been all too easy for him.

No—Victor was sending a message. It was a message for me, or for Roman, or for us both. And I continue down the trail with the ice-cold realization that my necklace can only protect one person at a time.

Three

I'm standing offstage in the main theater of the Lithia Theater Company watching Roman—I mean, Romeo—kneeling over Juliet, thinking she has just killed herself. Roman's hair has been cut short for the role, to make him look younger, and he does; he has captured the character perfectly as Romeo holds up a vial of poison, prepared to follow in Juliet's tragic footsteps:

> Eyes, look your last!
> Arms, take your last embrace! and, lips, O you
> The doors of breath, seal with a righteous kiss
> A dateless bargain to engrossing death!
> Come, bitter conduct; come, unsavoury guide!
> Thou desperate pilot, now at once run on
> The dashing rocks thy sea-sick weary bark!
> Here's to my love!

Roman puts the poison to his lips, and I think of the irony of the moment. How this man—this vampire—can never die, and how unimaginable it must be for him right now to pretend he is dying. But then, Roman's a great actor.

Romeo drains the vial and utters his last line.

O true apothecary!
Thy drugs are quick. Thus with a kiss I die.

As I watch his body go still, I feel thankful that I'll never know this moment for real—that Roman, for better or for worse, is here on earth to stay. And that I'll never have to be without him. At least, I don't think so—I've heard there are ways to kill vampires, but they can't be easy, or we wouldn't have to worry so much about Victor.

Lucy, standing next to me, leans over and whispers, "Romeo's not the brightest bulb on the tree, is he?"

It's true. The character of Romeo is more impulsive than thoughtful. If only he'd waited a few moments longer, he would have discovered that Juliet was alive, that she had taken a potion only to make her *appear* dead.

But timing is everything in drama—and in life. And Romeo arrived a bit too early.

"He's not hard on the eyes, though," I whisper back to Lucy.

I'm not here watching rehearsal because I'm an actor in this play; I'm actually a stagehand. My job is to shuffle furniture and props around between acts and scene changes. I hover in the wings waiting for the director to call for a prop to be moved. I enjoy being a part of the production, even though my role feels infinitesimal. At the same time, it's every little detail that makes all the shows here so good.

Lucy, whose dream is to be an actor, has been given a huge break. After seeing us perform at Lithia College, the director of this production asked us both to audition—a chance to work in a real, professional theater. *Romeo and Juliet* is a late addition to the normal theater schedule; usually the theater season winds down after the summer winds down, but this year—in part because the prodigal star Roman returned to town after a long absence—the theater decided to stage a special production of *Romeo and Juliet* for just three months. It was a lucky break not only for Roman, who needed a job and to prove himself again, but also for Lucy, who got the role of Nurse—a verbose, bawdy, and, at times, over-bearing character. As Lucy herself will admit, she was a perfect fit.

I auditioned for Juliet, but I knew I was facing steep odds. I'd played Isabella in *Measure for Measure* at the college, but I think I'd gotten lucky somehow, not only to have gotten the part but to have pulled it off. Isabella was the perfect character for me at just the right time in my life, and I think that's how I did it. I learned that I love acting, but I also learned that I'm not so much a natural actor as really good at channeling my own energy. I was nervous during my Juliet audition, and I knew even as I was reading my lines that I'd never get the part.

I'm still planning to minor in drama at the college, though. If I'm going to major in environmental studies, it will help to have acting skills. When you know your life is going to be made up of fighting to save land, and animals, and all the other things that need saving, it helps to know how to face an audience, to develop the poise you learn so well by being onstage.

For the time being, though, I don't mind being backstage. The girl who won the role of Juliet, Christine Arbor, is a professional actor. She's as young as I am but has been in movies and television since she was ten. She'd also played Juliet in other productions and already knew most of the lines by heart. I study her every moment I can, watching how she prepares herself for the role, how she carries herself. She *is* Juliet when she steps on that stage.

I have to admit I watch her closely because I'm a bit jealous when I see her and Roman lock lips, or gaze into each other's eyes. I have to keep reminding myself that they're excellent actors because they sure look like they're enjoying themselves. In one scene, Romeo wears only a skimpy pair of pajama bottoms and struts around stage half-naked, and Juliet's eyes follow his every move.

Yet I know in my heart that Roman only has eyes for me. I'm not sure I'll ever understand why, but the fact that he changed his whole life around just to be with me is proof enough. But it's been good for him, too—giving up the killing has lightened him somehow, helped him move on a bit from all his past mistakes. He couldn't help who he was then—but he's become a new person with a new future. And when you live forever, the future is something you really need to be able to look forward to.

I still feel like we're the ultimate odd couple, Roman and me, maybe even real-life versions of Romeo and Juliet. The vampires are the Montagues and the humans are the Capulets, and Roman and I are caught between them—two tribes seemingly at odds. And Lithia is like Verona, whose residents only want peace. We know how Shakespeare's drama ends—and now, with Victor back in Lithia and looming around everywhere, I'm anxiously wondering how things will end up here. I hope it's along the lines of a Shakespearean comedy—which ends with a wedding—instead of a tragedy, which ends in death, usually a whole lot of it.

Despite our differences, Roman is more like me than most humans. He subsists on a plant-based diet, just like I do. We both love to go running in the woods. And I think we're both equally stubborn, which is sometimes a challenge when we want different things, like the fact that I want to train for Cloudline and he wants to keep me off that mountain and out of the woods.

Victor does frighten me, though I don't like to let Roman know how much. What's even worse is knowing that Victor frightens Alex and Roman, too; I tend to think of both of Alex and Roman as invincible—and maybe they are, at least physically speaking, but not emotionally. They've both lost a lot in their lives, and they don't want to lose any more.

Still, some things are stronger than fear—and for me, it's my love of the land. Victor may be determined to use me to punish Roman for giving up the life he was born into, for becoming a vegan vampire and living off the trees, living a life of peace—but I'll never give up on Lithia. And as long as Roman never gives up on me, we will persevere.

Right?

If only I could be so sure.

Even Alex, though he knows I've made my choice to be with Roman, is still worried. The two of them used to hate each other, and seeing them united in the common mission to protect me has been strange indeed. A few times, I've left for work in the morning only to find either Alex or Roman standing right there, looking a bit groggy from being there all night but ready to escort me wherever I'm headed. I've tried to resist their caretaking, but there's no doubt among any of us that Victor is out for blood. My blood. Even if it's only to hurt Roman and Alex.

I'm brought back out of my thoughts by Stan Bedford, the play's director, calling out for a five-minute break.

Roman walks off the stage toward me and Lucy. "What do you think?" he asks. "Was my demise believable?"

"Not bad," says Lucy. "It's the living part that needs some work." She studies his preternaturally pale face. "Do you *ever* get any vitamin D, Roman?"

Lucy, despite being my best friend, doesn't know there are vampires in Lithia. Let alone that I'm dating one.

Roman turns to me. "Remind me again, Katherine, how long I have to endure having Lucy as a fellow cast member?"

"Only three months and twelve days more." I smile at his growing attempts at humor, at getting along with me and my friends. I always have to remind myself that he is more than a century old—and even if you're not, it can be hard to keep up with Lucy and her banter.

He smiles back me and heads toward the dressing rooms.

Lucy rolls her eyes. "You two are so cute it's gross."

I shush her up and change the subject. No one here at the theater knows about my romance with Roman, and I made Lucy promise not to broadcast it, though she said they'd find out about it soon enough. Small towns. Small theater companies. *Secrets don't stay secret for very long*, she said, and she's right.

Four

It's lonely, having secrets, and the one I'm carrying with me is becoming a burden—I can feel it sapping my energy as I finish my shift at the running store. I have too few people to talk to about the danger facing Lithia—and each day the weight feels a bit heavier. I know in my heart that I can tell Lucy anything, but even when I'm most tempted to tell her about the vampires of Lithia, I hold back—mostly because there is nothing she can do, and it would only terrify her.

But part of me wants to tell anyway—because it could also save her life.

I don't want to bring it up with Roman again, or Alex—they both just worry about me whenever I talk about Victor. I'm lucky to have both of them looking after me, but it also makes me feel like a helpless girl—which I'm not.

I'm restocking a couple boxes of shoes when I suddenly remember someone I *can* talk to. Someone who knows about

Lithia's vampires, or thinks he does—which right now is good enough for me.

I finish up at the store and shout a quick good-bye to David on my way out the door. I rush to the office of the parks department, and I burst in just as the receptionist is trying to close up.

A little breathless—another reminder that it's been way too long since I've gone for a good, long run—I ask if Doug is still there. "He just left," she says, waving her hand toward the street.

"Thanks," I call over my shoulder as I rush out. I haven't seen Doug Gibson in a while, but as I scan the parking lot, I see a fit, round-faced guy climbing into a Jeep, and I race over. I tap my hand against the driver's side door just as he's about to pull away.

He cuts the engine and opens the door. "Kat! Is everything all right?"

I nod, still trying to catch my breath. "I just have a question for you, if you have a second."

"Sure, what's up?"

Now I'm hesitating—how do I explain that there are good vampires and bad vampires? That I'm in love with one of them and yet I want Doug's help in getting rid of another?

"Kat?"

Okay, here goes. "Remember—it was a long time ago—when you said you thought there were vampires here in Lithia?"

He narrows his eyes. "Why do you ask?"

I take a breath. "I think you're right."

He gets out of the Jeep, closes the door, and leans against it. "What makes you a believer all of a sudden?"

"I've seen one." In a rush, I remind him about all the unexplained deaths, but he doesn't need reminding; he's been keeping track. And then I tell him about seeing Victor in the hills, but of course I don't mention his name.

But Doug is shaking his head. "Look, Kat, I do believe there are vampires here in Lithia, but this doesn't makes sense. If this guy was the real deal, you wouldn't be standing here right now."

"I think I'm here because of this." I tug on the necklace around my neck and hold out the stone so Doug can see it. "This is what scared him off."

Doug peers at the necklace. "Looks like serpentine," he says. "Can I see it?"

Reluctantly, I take it off and hand it to him. He turns it over in his hand, examining it. "Yep, serpentine," he says, then hands it back. "Interesting. Why would that scare them off?"

"I don't know," I say. "But it's the only thing I know of that does."

"Why do you say that?"

I hesitate. "Well, you know—vampires evolve, like everyone else. I've just—read a lot about them, that's all. Here's one example—I've heard that garlic doesn't really deter them."

"The wooden stake through the heart?"

"I've never tried that," I say. "But I'm guessing all those old methods are no good anymore. Everything's different. They come out in daylight now. They aren't freaked out by garlic. Is there *anything* that kills them?"

"There is one thing," Doug says thoughtfully.

"What's that?"

"Fire."

"Really?" I'm doubtful. "That seems like another one of the old myths. Besides, half the town was on fire not so long ago, and this vampire's still up there."

"They know enough to be afraid of it," Doug says. "To outrun it. But if we can trap him—"

I shake my head. "We can't risk that. Not with the wildfire danger around here."

"Yeah, I know," he admits. "If that fire that just blew through the forests didn't do the trick, I'm not sure what will."

"So what should we do? We need to warn people."

"Bad idea," Doug says. "And I should know. I've been trying for years to get people to pay attention. I've nearly lost my job, twice, for shooting my mouth off. And I'm the local laughingstock over at Sully's Pub. Once you go around saying there are vampires out there, they figure you believe in Bigfoot and UFOs as well."

"Do you?"

"Of course. Look, you and I may be certain about vampires, but we need to have some sort of proof before we can go public."

"The dead bodies aren't proof enough?" But I know he's right. People will believe what they want to believe—and believing in bears harming humans is easier than believing in vampires.

"Give me some time to think," Doug says.

"We don't have time."

"Just a couple days. I'll come up with a plan."

Reluctantly, I agree. I don't have any other options.

"Meanwhile, be careful," Doug says.

"You, too."

He gets in his car and drives away. I touch my necklace, grateful once again that I have this to protect me. If only I could give one to everyone in town.

Five

The body remembers.

Even though it's been weeks since I last laced up my old running shoes, my legs know what to do, taking up their old familiar pace, my lungs springing to life as they breathe in the pine air, and soon I'm rambling back up into the hills toward the Lost Mine Trail.

I made sure my necklace was securely around my neck right before I entered the forest. As much as I'd have enjoyed running with Roman, he's at the theater—and as much as I've always loved running with Alex, I haven't talked much with him in a while, and I'm not sure exactly where we stand.

I'm surprised by how strong my legs are, given the time I've taken off from running. Maybe it's all the pent-up angst I've been feeling. And I can tell I'm off to a pace too fast to sustain for long, but I don't care. I feel free again. When I'm running, I can forget that there are dangers all around me—even here, where danger seems to loom largest. With my necklace bumping against my collarbone, I know I am safe.

I want to win Cloudline again. Winning that race the first time gave me the confidence I needed to face so many other fears in my life—and now, I want to feel that again. To face Victor. To face all I want to accomplish in school and in life. To face being in love with a vampire and the constant wonder of where it will lead us. It's a little disconcerting to think of the ways there might be to kill a vampire—it makes me realize how Roman and Alex are vulnerable, too. But then, nothing in life is certain, and I guess all of us are, in the end, vulnerable to something.

But knowing I'll be running the race gives me a newfound source of energy and a goal that is mine and mine alone. And I believe I can win it again. I want to prove that to myself. And, yes, I'd also like to prove it to Erica Summers. To put her back in her place. I can't help it. All runners want to be the first across that finish line.

This is what I love about running—you can run against others and you can run against yourself. Or, sometimes, you can do both at the same time, which is what I'll be doing in a few weeks. Which is actually what I'm doing even now.

I make sure that my route takes me not directly home but by my land, giving me a chance to check up on it.

My land.

I'm still getting used to calling it that. And I actually try *not* to refer to the land that way. Nobody truly owns the land. We are all just renters in the end, all just passing through. The trees, the oldest residents, should have the greatest right to it, not us.

But even if I don't see myself as owner of the land, I am definitely its caretaker. And right now, it needs a lot of care. From where I'm standing, it looks like a disaster area.

Although most of this land has been untouched for generations, a portion of it has been developed—at least, sort of. Ed Jacobs had gotten hold of it and had begun building a neighborhood of mansions up here when the fire roared through. And when Roman dug up all that gold from the secret mine entrance, he used some of it to buy back Jacobs's partially developed—and now totally fire-ravaged—property. By then, Jacobs didn't want it anymore.

There is still a sign at the entrance to the property, past the blackened chain-link fence that was flattened in sections by fire trucks, next to a concrete driveway that dead-ends at a charred skeleton of a house. The sign reads Highland Hills, and the view up here is grand. Down below you can see the town, the theater complex, the Manzanita Hotel towering over the main street.

My dad wanted to have a house here. He'd tricked me into signing the Horton property over to him so he could sell it to Ed Jacobs, thinking he'd make a fortune. And he might have—but then Jacobs left him out of the deal altogether.

I last saw my dad not far from here, the night he found out he was penniless again. And he was drunk again, and I was hurrying up the hill to try to find Roman. And then the fire started.

My father ran into the flames, looking for me. And I can picture him doing so, his one great, brave act in life, trying to save his only child. And in death he left me something that I will keep with me forever—his act of bravery makes me realize that I want to live a brave life myself, not just occasionally but always. And part of that, I think, is making the best use of these devastated acres, though I'm not sure where exactly to begin. All I see is a cemetery of charred wood-frame structures and concrete foundations. On one lot, only a chimney remains. Scattered around are piles of stones and bricks. I glimpse the burned-out hull of a construction truck.

When I hear dogs barking, I whirl around, heart thumping. No one but me has a reason to be up here.

But what I see is a welcome sight: Alex approaching—or rather, being dragged along like a water skier by the leashes of four excited dogs.

"Hey there," he calls over the yelps of his pack.

I lean down to pet each of the dogs, all falling over themselves in their eagerness to say hello. "I thought you only had two dogs," I say.

He smiles sheepishly. "I adopted two more last week. It's a sickness, I know. But since I've been working at the hospital I've been overwhelmed with strays."

"Hospital?"

"Animal hospital," he says. "Over near the highway. Didn't I tell you?"

"No," I say. "That's great." Then I venture, "I guess it has been a while since we last talked."

"I know," he says. "I'm sorry. It's been crazy. Two weeks ago I left the Food Co-Op and began working part-time at the animal hospital. As a vet assistant."

"Wow," I say. "I didn't even know you had a medical background."

"I don't need one to be an assistant," he says, "but I do want to become a tech eventually, and I'll need certification and a license for that. Maybe I'll even become a veterinarian one day."

I feel my smile grow bigger at the thought. "That would be perfect for you, Alex."

He smiles back. "Now that I'm there, I can't imagine working anywhere else. The money's tight, but I think I'll go to full-time in a month or two."

"It sounds like a calling."

"It is."

I look at the happy dogs tethered to him, all looking at him with adoration, tongues hanging out, tails wagging. "But you're going to have to stop bringing home strays," I say with a laugh. "If you adopted two more dogs after only two weeks working part-time, you're in real trouble."

He smiles. "You're still my favorite stray."

I *was* a stray when we met, lost and alone and hungry in Lithia. Alex had brought me food, protected me from Roman's still-dangerous ways, and basically saved my life. "I was probably one of the more pathetic strays you've ever encountered."

"I've seen far worse," he says. "And you were definitely the cutest."

It's then that I realize how close together we're standing, with only the dogs between us, and I also realize how much I still care for Alex. It's such a different kind of love, so different from what I feel for Roman—but I feel it all the same.

And I know that I need to step away before I'm tempted to do something insane. Like lean over and kiss him.

I take a step backward and change the subject. "So, you wouldn't be in the market for some slightly charred timber, by any chance?"

He looks around with a sigh. "This is quite a mess."

"I thought I could clear it all away to plant trees again, but I didn't realize how many concrete foundations had been poured already."

"Maybe you could reuse the foundations."

"For what?"

"I don't know. Build a nature center, maybe? Make them into cabins or classrooms to teach people about the land?"

I stare at it all and feel overwhelmed. So much burned timber needs to be piled up and trucked away just to begin to get at the wood that can be reused, to begin to assess what's left.

"I wouldn't know where to begin," I say.

Alex seems to be reading my mind. He tethers the dogs to a fence post, strips off his sweatshirt, and slaps his hands together.

"I've got a few hours before work. What can I do?"

"This is going to take much more than a few hours."

He reaches down and picks up one end of a charred two-by-four. "Give me a hand," he says. "Might as well start somewhere. An hour's start is better than no start."

I reach down and grab the other end, and we carry the wood to a small pile of burnt wood pieces that, as we work, begins to grow into a huge pile.

After a while, I realize how thirsty I am—and remember that I'd been on a long run before we got to work, and Alex had been on a long walk with the dogs, and neither of us had brought any water. We gather the dogs and move under the shade of a half-built home, the roof still largely intact.

"So how's Roman?" Alex asks, his eyes cast downward, at the ears of one of the dogs he's petting.

"Good," I say.

"You've been seeing a lot of him lately?"

"Yeah, I guess."

"I suppose him giving up meat, going vegan like me, was a sign that anyone can change. I never thought he would."

I can't help but smile. "It's hard to believe. Especially after he took me to a steakhouse on our first date."

"So he's back in Lithia for good, I suppose?"

"Looks that way. He moved out of the hotel and into a little house in the Pioneer District."

"Near your place?"

"Pretty close, yeah."

Alex looks up, then reaches for my hand. "Kat," he says, "I know you're with Roman now—but if there is ever still a chance for us, you promise you'll let me know?"

"I promise," I say, slowly, not sure what I'm promising. In a way, there will always be a chance for Alex and me because I will always love Alex. Yet I also love Roman, and I've made my choice, and I can't have it both ways. I suppose I chose Roman because I know Alex and I can be friends, that we will always be friends, at the very least—but Roman and I have never been anything but in love. I've loved him and I've hated him, but I've never been just friends with him.

We get back to work. Alex finds a few abandoned tools, all charred, and he takes an ax to a charred wall. The ax slices with ease through the thick wood. I follow and stand behind him, out of the danger zone.

"You have a knack for this," I say.

"Well," he says, then hesitates. "Truth be told, I used to do this for a living."

"You? I thought you *protected* trees."

"I do. Now. But a long time ago I was a different person."

"How different?"

41

He smiles sadly and puts down the ax. "I was a logger."

"*What?* I don't believe it." A logger—just like my dad. Back when they met, Alex had given me such a hard time about my dad destroying trees, being part of the ongoing destruction of the planet.

It's true, what Lucy says. *Secrets don't stay secret for very long.*

"It was more than a hundred years ago," Alex says, reminding me again of the difference between us, between me and him and Roman. "I worked chopping down old-growth forests. Those were the only jobs around here back then—logging or gold digging."

"I know." I don't tell him that Roman had worked in the mines, but maybe he already knows. These two were such a big part of the land back then, within it and on it and tearing it apart. I'm still trying to process what Alex is telling me as he continues.

"I didn't have the stomach for working underground," Alex says. "And back then, I wasn't truly aware of what I was doing. I worked in the redwoods."

The redwoods—where Alex had first told me what he really is. He'd told me how he'd watched them grow over the decades— he loves those trees. I can hardly believe what I'm hearing.

"I cleared hundreds of those amazing trees," Alex continues with a sigh. "Back then, it took ten men to cut through a redwood, chipping away at the edges for days. They were so big, so old— you look at these trees, and by comparison they're so small. And of course we were arrogant, thought we were so strong—like it was us versus the trees."

"How come you never told me this?"

"I was always too embarrassed. Ashamed. I was young and ignorant and desperate for a little money. Back then, I had traveled a long way to get here, thinking I'd get rich."

"You were just like my dad," I say. "You were so hard on him—and all this time, you had done the same thing."

"I know, Kat," Alex says. "And honestly, I think I reacted so strongly to your dad's work because it brought up the shame of what I used to do. Like your dad, I didn't have a lot of options, and somehow I told myself that made it okay. My own dad was a dirt-poor Kansas farmer, and they needed the money I could make out here. So I did what I had to do. I chopped down the very trees that later saved my life."

He shakes his head. "You know, it was strange back then. I had moments when I looked up at these trees, these monuments to time, and I felt so guilty. So cruel. I knew even then that what I was doing was wrong. The trees couldn't fight back. They were just standing there, like they had for centuries, living their lives, not bothering a soul, cleaning our air, giving nests to birds, making the world a better place just by being alive. And then we arrived with our axes and saws and train cars, and we left behind miles and miles of stumps."

I feel tears in my eyes, and I put my hand on his. "What convinced you to stop?"

"We were about ready to fell a tree, one of the largest we'd cut. I stepped back and looked at it, and I swear I saw a face in the bark looking back at me." He looks out across the trees. "I know it was just the patterns in the wood, or the sweat in my eyes, or something like that—but I felt I saw it. It was like that tree was looking directly at me, even speaking to me, and what it was telling me was that I needed to stop."

He squeezes my hand. "We all had contracts, so quitting wasn't an option—but I decided to go home to my family anyway. Not that I wanted to—I didn't know how I was going to explain myself to them—but I had enough for train fare home, and one night I snuck out and headed for the nearest town."

He goes silent.

"What happened?"

"My boss happened," Alex says. "He wasn't a man you could sneak out on. I was one of his best workers, one of the strongest, the most productive. He tracked me down that night, before I could even get very far, and he offered me"—Alex pauses—"a different career path, I guess you would say."

"I don't understand."

"He said I had two choices. I could either die right then of a gunshot wound to the head—and he held up the gun to prove it—or I could live forever."

I feel fear prickling the back of my neck, a sudden chill. "Who was this boss?"

"Victor."

I feel a wave of shock go through my body. "Just like Roman."

Alex nods. "Victor always wins. That's why Roman and I are worried about you. You think you can beat him, or at least avoid him, but you can't."

"But you broke free of him, right? You became vegan."

"I did—but only because he chose to let me go," Alex says. "I'm not like Roman. Roman was Victor's heir apparent. I think Victor always hoped Roman would do away with me, but now that Roman has broken free, too, it's not going to end pretty."

"There must be a way." I'm glad I've got Doug on the case, though I'm not about to tell Alex about it. Or Roman, for that matter.

"Well, I think there's hope," Alex says. "The world is changing. What I did, giving up the violence—this idea is spreading. For years, Victor ignored me—he could ignore me as long as Roman stayed true. Now he has to deal not only with me but with Roman. And all the others who are following behind us."

"Is it worth it, though?" I ask. "When none of us are safe?"

Alex looks at me. "Have you thought of leaving town, Kat? It would be safe that way, you know. Victor sees this as his home turf. If you go, he'll leave you alone forever."

"But it's my home turf, too. Why should I be the one to leave? He took my land. Indirectly, he took my parents. I'd rather die first."

"Kat, that's the point. Everyone dies if they try to fight Victor."

"But my own safety's not enough. I can't leave this town knowing he's preying on people. We have to do something. There has to be a way to get rid of him, a weakness."

"If Victor has a weakness, I haven't seen it."

I think of my conversation with Doug. "What about fire?"

"Fire," Alex repeats. "I don't know, Kat. Of course, all vampires are vulnerable to fire—including Victor. Including me—and you, for that matter. But because he knows this, you'll never get him near a flame. He's too fast, too elusive to risk getting burnt."

"He sleeps, doesn't he?"

"Like a bird sleeps. Lightly. Easily awoken. Never truly asleep."

"So if we can't sneak up on Victor, we have to trick him somehow. Lure him toward us." I'm thinking aloud—not making plans with Alex but making plans, in my mind, with Doug.

"Don't be crazy, Kat," Alex says, the look on his face one of deep concern. "He will beat you, in the end. You could have a dozen of those necklaces on, and Victor would find a way around them."

The evening is coming earlier now that the season is changing. Exhausted from all our work, Alex and I head down the hill. He and the dogs escort me to the edge of town, and then we go our separate ways.

When Alex is well out of sight, I take a wide detour. I walk through a fancy neighborhood filled with beautiful homes, until I find myself staring at an immense, ornate house—a mansion, really—a mansion I once spent a very glamorous evening in a long time ago.

Victor's mansion.

Roman used to live in Victor's house, which should more accurately be called a castle. Nestled high above Lithia, the gothic mansion looks like something out of ancient Europe, with gargoyles and turrets and the feeling that it has always been here, since the beginning of time. In the ballroom of this house, Roman and I had danced at a Halloween party. And, come to think of it, Alex and I had danced, too.

Ever since Roman had his falling-out with Victor and left so abruptly, the house has deteriorated quickly; all the staff must've left, too. The lawn is overgrown with weeds, the windows covered in ivy. It has a cold, vacant feel, and it's hard to believe that anyone lives there—or has ever lived there.

Roman has told me that Victor is still there, and knowing this—that someone is living in this dark, desolate house—makes it all the creepier. Now, at dusk, I look up at it from the street, and there is not a single light on in the whole place. And yet Victor is in there somewhere—or so I assume. Or hope. Because if he's in there, at least he's not out preying on some innocent human.

I feel a dread deep in my stomach when I look at this house. A feeling that I must go in there if I'm going to put an end to this nightmare. But I don't know where I'll find the courage to push open that front door, to take on Victor in his element. Up in the forest, at least, I feel like I'm in my own element—and at least I can always run away, escape. But in Victor's lair, I have a feeling there is no such thing as escape.

Six

When Mr. Ramsey comes through the door I try not to show my impatience. Mr. Ramsey is a gentleman in his seventies who comes in once every other week and tries on practically every pair of shoes in the store.

And he never buys a thing.

I know I shouldn't complain. Ever since I returned to Lithia, the Lithia Runners store has been my home away from home. When I first moved back to town, David and his fiancée, Stacey, gave me my first big break, offering me part-time work and letting me rent the cottage behind their house. I never thought I could be so lucky.

That is, until that day that Stacey and I went running into the hills and Stacey was taken by a vampire—by Roman, I later learned. It took me a long time to forgive him, but his becoming vegan is proof that he has put the violence behind him. He gives me hope that everyone is capable of change.

David still assumes, like the rest of Lithia, that Stacey's death was another bear attack. Only Doug knew the truth back then—and I'm glad I've confided in him at last.

Still, the weight of knowing the truth, of wondering whether I could have done something to protect her, is a heavy burden to bear.

Thanks to David, I kept working at the store, and he even got me started at Lithia College, paying for part-time classes as long as I did my job and kept my grades up. He was like the dad I never had—someone who cared about my well-being, my future.

But I know David has a future of his own to think about—a future that may not always include me as an employee and tenant. I suspect that I'm going to have to leave the nest sometime soon—David's new girlfriend, Kendra, is working in the store full-time, and they usually only need me a couple times a week. Plus, the two of them are becoming quite serious; they often ask me to close up so they can go to dinner or to the theater, and I can hardly remember the last time David was so happy. It was a long time ago, back when Stacey was alive.

I bring out another pair of shoes for Mr. Ramsey, but as usual, he can't seem to make up his mind. I once asked David if Mr. Ramsey has dementia, but David knows his kids, and they say he is the picture of health. After all, he's here to buy running shoes, so he's clearly fit, and, according to David, he does have the money to pay for them. Apparently, he's just insanely fussy and doesn't do very well with making decisions.

David gave up waiting on him long ago and often retreats to the back room when Mr. Ramsey enters the store. Even Kendra has learned to disappear, so I'm the one left to assist him. I'm beginning to look at this as a challenge, like Cloudline. One of these days I'm going to close a sale.

Unfortunately, tonight I am hoping to leave early for a date with Roman.

"Well, better luck next time, I guess," I tell Mr. Ramsey, standing up and collecting the half-dozen opened shoe boxes.

"I thought you said you had a few new pairs that had just come in."

"Did I?" I take a quick glance at my watch. Any other day, I'd have brought out every pair, but it's getting late. "You know, I did check on those, and it turns out your size isn't available."

"Oh."

"So, thanks for coming in," I tell him, standing up with my arms full of shoe boxes.

He stands slowly. "What about those walking shoes?" He points to another wall. "I'd like to try those on, please."

I sigh. "Hold on."

I dash into the back, wondering where Kendra and David are and how I can get them to rescue me. The theater is dark tonight, and Roman invited me out to a vegan restaurant in town—the *only* vegan restaurant in town, actually. It's new, and I've decided it will be my mission to keep the place in business.

It's only a few blocks away, and if I don't change out of my work outfit—running clothes—I still have a chance of making it on time. But as I look around the storeroom, I see a mess of opened shoe boxes scattered about. Things are picking up in anticipation of Cloudline, and yet David and Kendra have been glued at the hip and hardly aware of anything around them, let alone that David has a business to run and that his only other employee is already working two jobs and taking classes at the college.

When I get back to the front with Mr. Ramsey's walking shoes, he is standing near the door. "You know, maybe I'll just come back when you get those other shoes in. I really need running shoes, not walking shoes."

"Okay, then," I say with a sigh. "I'll see you next week."

I watch Mr. Ramsey leave, then I rush to clean up the remaining opened boxes on the main floor.

Finally the place is looking decent, and I shout toward the back, where I think David and Kendra are in the office. I've learned not to walk in on them. "I'm heading out the front," I call out. "You want me to lock up?"

David appears. "Kat, do you have a minute?"

"What is it?" I ask.

"I have to talk to you about something."

He looks so serious that I'm beginning to worry. "I know I was a bit short with Mr. Ramsey," I say, "but I'm really late for a date with Roman, and I—"

David laughs. "Don't worry, this isn't about Mr. Ramsey. You have the patience of a saint with that man."

I'm relieved. "What is it, then? Is everything okay?"

"Very okay," David says, and he smiles. "I just wanted you to be the first to know that Kendra and I are getting married."

"Really?" I feel a smile of my own spread across my face. This certainly explains why they've been so lovey-dovey lately.

"I asked, and, fortunately, she said yes." He rubs his hand across his brow in a *phew* gesture.

I throw my arms around him. "I'm so happy for you. For both of you."

"It's funny," he says. "I never thought I'd meet someone I could love as much as Stacey. But life keeps you guessing."

"Stacey would be happy for you," I say.

"You think so?" I can see a hint of wistfulness in his eyes.

"I know it. She would want you to be happy."

He smiles. "I think you're right. And I am."

Kendra emerges from the back and gives David a look. "You were supposed to wait for me."

"I couldn't wait."

"Well, you better get used to following my orders." She gives him a playful nudge and winks at me.

"So, when's the date?" I ask.

"Soon," Kendra says. "But it's going to be very simple, outdoors in the park. Just a few friends and family—and that includes you, Kat. Plus one."

"Plus one," I say. I've never had a *plus one* before.

"Speaking of, who will you bring—Alex or Roman?" Kendra asks.

Kendra is all too aware of my early romance with Roman, the breakup, then my romance with Alex, and that breakup, too.

"Roman," I say. "Roman and I are together now. For good."

"Perfect," she says, "because David was going to ask him to be a groomsman."

David smiles. "Roman's been one of my best customers over the years."

"And I hope you'll be a bridesmaid," Kendra says.

"I would love to."

I race into the restaurant and slide into the chair across from Roman's. "I have a great excuse for being late, I promise." But when I tell Roman the news, he doesn't seem surprised.

"I had a feeling David was getting ready to propose."

"How could you tell?"

"I saw him coming out of the jewelry store near the plaza last week," Roman says.

"That doesn't mean anything. He could've been buying a bracelet for Kendra, or a pair of earrings."

"Sometimes you just know these things," Roman says.

"Well, the older, the wiser," I say, and he smiles.

"So," he asks, "are you happy for David and Kendra?"

"Of course! What kind of question is that?"

"Sometimes marriage changes things, Katherine. Not only for the two getting married, but for everyone around them."

I look at him. "So have you ever been married, Roman?"

"No, Katherine. I never had the chance to get married."

There's a sadness in his eyes, and I remember the story he'd told me about how he became what he is—he'd been buried in a mine, and Victor had promised to save him. And he did, but not in the way Roman expected.

"Did you *want* to get married?"

"There was a young woman at the time," he says. "But of course, it became impossible, and she moved on."

"So, vampires can't get married?"

"It is incompatible with who we are," he says. "No bride would survive her wedding night."

"But what about now? You're a vegan now."

"Now," he says, "everything is different." He looks at me. "What about you, Katherine? Do you ever think about marriage?"

"I don't know," I confess. "I never thought about it because my own parents weren't happy. But, seeing David and Kendra— maybe it's not so bad after all."

A waiter comes by to take our orders, and I realize I haven't even looked at my menu. And it's not until I look back up at Roman, at the expression on his face, that I begin to wonder why he is so interested in marriage.

Seven

I'm onstage, staring out at the lights. But there are no lines for me to recite. No marks to hit. No costumes to wear.

Instead, I am moving stage props around. I'm dressed in black, the standard outfit for stagehands, and along with two others, I stand and await instructions from Stan, who's seated in the middle of the orchestra section talking in his headset to the lighting director.

The actors are not here today, just us stagehands. And while being a stagehand is decidedly less glamorous than being an actor, I enjoy playing a different role in this production—learning about how the stage works, how lighting is set according to scenes and backdrops. Far above me, I hear feet walking across metal platforms as lights are repositioned, filters added or removed. At one moment I'm bathed in green, then blue, and now dark red.

I see movement at the rear of the theater, someone standing by the door. I squint into the darkness, thinking Roman has come to meet me—it's someone dressed in black, which is practically the only color Roman ever wears. The red light fades enough for me to focus, and my stomach sinks when I realize who I'm staring at.

And who is staring at me.

Victor.

He is smiling, and what this tells me is that something evil is about to happen. To Victor, people are nameless; they are just meals, some better than others. It's the same way a human may look at a burger and have no concept that it was once a beautiful cow, a living being as sweet as a dog. No connection. No empathy.

I know that Victor can't attack me in front of all these people, or at least I assume as much. But could I be wrong? Could he really hurt me in broad daylight, in the middle of a lighting rehearsal?

Somewhere underneath my black turtleneck is my necklace, and I reach up to make sure it is still there. If Victor has no plans to attack me, then what is he doing here at the theater? He knows where to find me, after all—he has no reason to be here.

I hear a creak up above, and suddenly it's all too obvious. The lights.

I look up just in time to see the light beam falling, heading straight for the top of my head.

—⁓—

When I come to, I see a circle of faces floating above me. Then I remember where I am—not exactly where I was a few moments ago, onstage, but on the ground next to the stage. Did I manage to dive out of the way, or did the light beam knock me out?

"What happened?" I ask.

Stan's face comes into focus in front of me. "Kat, can you hear me?"

I nod, feeling an ache in my head.

"Can you move?" he asks. "Try your arms and legs."

I wiggle my toes, then bend my knees, reaching my hands down to touch them. I hear sighs of relief. I sit up, and Stan reaches down to help me to my feet. Next to me is a long beam loaded with lights, most of them crushed into tiny shards of glass. I can't believe that almost landed squarely on top of me.

"That was close," I say.

"It sure was," Stan says. "You saw it at the very last second and narrowly missed getting hit. Though I imagine you'll be a little sore after leaping off the stage. I'd like you to see a doctor before coming in tomorrow."

"Okay," I say, then look up.

Stan follows my gaze. "A cable must have snapped," he says. "I'll get someone over here to look at it. It's a miracle you weren't hurt."

It is a miracle, though not the type that Stan is thinking of. I glance toward the rear of the theater again, but Victor is no longer there. It's obvious he was behind this, though no one would ever believe me, even if I could prove it. I don't even know if I should tell Alex and Roman—they'd believe me, but it would only cause them more worry.

I think about Doug and realize that this is not your typical vampire behavior; Victor is getting even more dangerous, going after me where I work. I no longer have to watch myself only in the hills but everywhere—and it's not just me but everyone around me who could end up in the line of fire. I'm going to have to do a better job of staying alert.

"Lucky timing, I guess," I say, finally responding to Stan.

Stan laughs. "The difference between tragedy and comedy is all in the timing."

Eight

I leave the theater, and though Stan thinks I need to see a doctor, instead I retreat to my land. I know I'm fine, and right now the best thing for my health is to be alone. To catch my breath and think about what to do next.

I know it's not such a wise idea to be heading alone into the hills after what just happened, but on the other hand, what just happened is proof that nowhere is safe—so why not go where I feel most peaceful? At least out here, by myself, I'm not putting anyone else in harm's way. I'm still reeling with the thought that the light beam could've fallen not only on me but on any other member of the crew—we were all very lucky. And I wonder how much time I have before this luck starts to run out.

I sit down on the edge of one of the concrete foundations. It's black with soot, but at least I'm still wearing black from the rehearsal. I jump when I hear a voice behind me.

"I had a feeling I'd find you here."

I turn and look up to see Roman standing there.

"Can't you at least try to sound human when you sneak up on me?" I ask. "Like rustle some leaves or something?"

He smiles. "I'm sorry, Katherine. I wanted to see you as quickly as possible. I wasn't thinking."

"You heard what happened?"

He nods.

"It was Victor," I say.

Roman takes a seat next to me and puts an arm around me. "I was worried it might have been," he says.

"I figured that since I was wearing this necklace I'd be safe. But you were right—Victor's just going to go after me in new ways. He's looking for some way that doesn't involve him getting too close."

"Victor is very smart," Roman says, "which also makes him very dangerous."

"Is he ever going to leave me alone?"

Roman shakes his head. "You're the symbol of this new battle," he says. "The battle between us and them."

"Them?" I say. "How many more of them are there?"

"I don't know for certain. Vampires are territorial, and we can cover a great deal of land. Victor has lorded over this region for centuries. The only vampires here are those he creates. And he is afraid of losing them."

"Like he lost you and Alex."

"I'm afraid so."

"So he'll never leave," I say. "It's him or me, isn't it?"

Roman squeezes my shoulder. "Him or us, Katherine. You are not alone in this."

Like Alex, Roman suffered so much because of Victor. More than a hundred years ago, Roman was just a young miner, someone drawn to the gold rush like so many thousands of others. And, like so many thousands of others, he found very little gold. Mostly, he ended up broke, with lungs full of dirt and smoke from the lanterns they used to find their way through the muck and rock. And so when the ceilings collapsed and men around him died, Roman was content to say good-bye to the world as well. Until Victor appeared in the darkness and promised a way to safety. Victor, the owner of the mines, and, to Roman, a god of sorts. Wealthy beyond belief. Power beyond control. How could Roman have said no?

"Can I ask you a question about the mines?"

"Of course."

"Do you think that earthquake was an accident? The one that closed up the mines?"

Professor Lindquist, my former environmental studies professor, believes that the earth will defend itself, and I think he is probably right. I'm wondering now whether Roman agrees.

"I am quite certain few things in life are accidents, Katherine. Today being a good example. With Victor, there are no coincidences, and certainly no accidents."

I think of another question. "Down in the mines—why did Victor target you? When there were so many others?"

"He told me he selected me because of my strength. He said I had the potential to be as strong as he was."

"Alex said you were Victor's heir apparent. That he was grooming you to take over."

Roman nods. "That's right."

"And I've ruined all that."

"You've changed all that," Roman says. "There's a difference. You made me something better. And Victor hates the idea that others like me may wish to change. So many others have lived lives of misery and guilt, and once they realize that they don't have to live off the lives of others—well, it is easy to see why this makes Victor so uneasy. This is a powerful idea."

"An idea whose time has come," I say.

"This idea, to Victor, is like a virus. And everyone who carries it must be quarantined."

"You mean killed," I say.

Roman nods.

"So," I ask, "how do we stop him?"

"If I knew how, I would have done so already. I am strong and fast, but Victor has history on his side."

"History?"

"I've never dueled to the death with one of my own. But Victor—he's battled vampires on every continent. He knows every deception, every trick, and, because he made me, he knows my weaknesses."

"You mean me," I say.

Roman says nothing.

"He's not going to stop until he kills me. Right?"

"Katherine, Victor's not going to stop until he kills us both."

Nine

I'm asleep in my cottage when a noise awakens me, or maybe it's a dream. I sit up in bed and listen. It's raining—that's what must've woken me, the sound of the rain on the roof. I sigh and lie back down.

My eyes scan the ceiling in the dark, and then I turn toward the window. It's pitch-black outside—no moon, no streetlights—and suddenly I feel very alone, and this paralyzes me under my blanket. Normally I enjoy my solitude, but all of a sudden I am aware of how very alone I am in this tiny one-room house of mine—especially knowing that if Victor were here, he would make no noise at all.

I try to close my eyes again and take a deep breath, but I can't stop my heart from beating like a rabbit's, and suddenly I'm burning up under the blanket, like I'm halfway through a run up Mount Lithia.

I throw off my blanket and let the room's cool air wash over me. I think of my necklace and how grateful I am to have it protecting me. I reach up to wrap my fingers around it, knowing it'll make me feel safe.

My fingers find nothing but my own bare skin. My necklace is gone.

I sit up again in the darkness—and then I see him. Two burning red coals staring back at me at the foot of my bed.

"Missing something?" In one horrible, final gesture, Victor rises up above me, then dives back down, fangs bared.

I begin to scream, as loudly as I possibly can—so loudly that I wake myself up.

A dream.

Only a dream.

Drenched in sweat, I blink at the bedside clock. It's 4:15, and now I'm wide awake. I reach up to my neck and clutch the serpentine in my hand.

It was only a dream—this time. What about next time? What if I lose this necklace, or if Victor does manage to get his hands on it?

This is the third nightmare I've had this week. I can't go on like this.

I try to relax, to get back to sleep, but my mind is spinning. Not only do I have to worry about Victor, but I've got a life to live, too; today I have rehearsal, then my class at the college, then a shift at the running store, and homework. And I still hope to get some Cloudline training in, but where that will fit I have no idea.

I lie in bed until sunlight finds its way through the windows. I get dressed in black for rehearsal, and I pack my books for school. I can't stop thinking about my nightmare, but when I emerge from the cottage, the rain has subsided, and the air smells full of life. And for the moment, my nightmare was just that—a bad dream.

Still, I know that the nightmares won't end—nor will my real-life fears—until something is done. And I decide to stop by the parks department on my way to rehearsal.

—⁓—

Doug is in the office, at his desk, and I step in and close the door behind me.

He looks alarmed. "Kat. Is something wrong?"

"I don't have a lot of time right now," I say.

"What happened?"

"Nothing—yet. But I have a terrible feeling something will."

He lets out a sigh. "I know. I've been thinking a lot about what you said."

"And?"

He opens a desk drawer and shuffles through some papers. Pulling out one page from all the rest, he holds it up. "Since using fire isn't possible," he says, "and you don't think a wooden stake will work, I've come up with this."

He puts the paper down on the desk, and I lean over to take a look. It's a drawing of some sort of knife.

"What's this?"

"A blade," Doug says, "made of serpentine."

"Where'd you get this?"

"I drew it." Doug turns back to the sheaf of papers and riffles through them for another moment. He hands me another couple of pages, all filled with drawings—of knives, stakes, various weapons blunt and sharp.

"You want to make a weapon of serpentine?"

Doug nods. "To put through this guy's heart. I figure if you wearing that thing is enough to scare him off, this is probably the only way to kill him."

I look at the drawings. "Not a bad idea," I admit. "The question is—how are you going to pull it off? You'll never get close enough."

"That's the hard part," Doug says. "Somehow I'll need to lure him close enough to stab him with it."

"In the exact right spot in his chest," I add. "Sorry, Doug, but this sounds a bit too risky to me."

"I know it sounds that way," he says, "but there's no other choice."

"You can let me help," I say. "This vampire—he's come after me before. He will again. If I'm the one to lure him out, then you can—"

But Doug is shaking his head. "No way, Kat. Besides, he knows you have the necklace. He won't try harming you again."

"Yes, he will."

Doug narrows his eyes at me. "What makes you say that?"

I hesitate. "I—I could see it in his eyes, that's all." I shudder, but it's not for effect; picturing Victor's eyes gives me a chill for real. "He's just so—evil."

"Which is why it's better if I show up alone. He won't suspect I have any serpentine, or any weapon at all for that matter, and I'll be ready for him. When he comes after me, I'll make my move."

"He's too fast for you."

"Let's not fuss over the details right now, Kat. First I need to find enough serpentine to create this thing."

"Where will you find it?"

"I know where to look."

"Is there a lot of it around here?" I have a vision of providing everyone in town with serpentine.

"Could be," he says, "but I don't know how much. I'm hoping I can find enough to make what I need." He holds up two pages, one in each hand. "What do you think?" he asks. "The stake or the blade?"

"Something sharp," I tell him. "You won't have enough time to think, and probably barely enough time to react at all. You need something you can use instantly."

He's looking at me again, suspiciously. "Is there something you aren't telling me, Kat? You seem to know an awful lot about this vampire."

"It's just—when someone comes that close to killing you, you remember everything," I manage to say. "It's still there, in my mind, every time I close my eyes."

His look turns sympathetic. "Sorry," he says. "Don't worry, I'll get him."

"I want to be there. I really think I can help you."

He shakes his head. "Not now, Kat. First things first. Why don't you come back next week? I should be able to find a big stone by then and will have something carved up and almost ready. We can talk strategy then."

Relief floods through me, and I nod. "Sounds great. Hurry, though. We need to act sooner than later."

"I know," he says. "No one knows that more than me."

Lucy and I are walking to campus after the morning rehearsal.

The weather is turning, and I can smell autumn in the golden leaves that crunch beneath our feet. This is my favorite time of year.

I pick up a leaf and hold it out to Lucy. She's been asking why I was late to rehearsal that morning, and I've been trying not to answer.

She takes the leaf, then tosses it into the air and watches it fall back to the ground. "Late night? Roman keep you up?"

"I wasn't even with Roman last night."

"Then who?"

"No one," I say with a laugh. "I just didn't sleep well. The rain woke me up, and I overslept."

I know Lucy sees right through me, and I change the subject. "Great rehearsal this morning," I tell her.

"That Nurse sure does talk a mean streak," Lucy says. "I wish she'd shut up once in a while just so I'd have fewer lines to memorize."

"You don't really mean that, do you?"

"No, of course not. I love shooting my mouth off up there. She's a great character, so brash and bawdy."

"I'm amazed you even had to audition," I say. "It's like Shakespeare had you in mind when he wrote it."

"If he really did have me in mind, I'd have been born in England like five hundred years ago."

"Women weren't even allowed to act in his plays back then, remember?" I say. "He was seeing into the future."

It's her turn to laugh. "I wish you had a role, too. It would be a lot more fun."

"It's fine. I have my hands full as it is. Besides, I like skulking around backstage."

"I bet you do." Lucy grins. "So, that Mercutio is a hottie."

"I'm surprised it took you so long to notice."

"Oh, trust me, I noticed. I was just being discreet."

"Right—like you even know the meaning of the word. So, is he single?"

"Yep. We actually bumped into each other in the park yesterday and walked along the creek for a bit. He's from LA. He loves dogs and yoga, and he thinks I'm hilarious."

I'm smiling, picturing Lucy in the park, wandering the trails with Mercutio—whose real name I can't remember—and suddenly another image comes to mind: Victor, hurtling down from the trees.

I feel a wave of nausea roll through me. I don't even realize I've stopped walking until Lucy stops and looks back at me.

"Hey! What's the matter?"

"Nothing, sorry."

She shrugs her shoulders in one of her dramatic Lucy gestures. "Oh, not to worry. It's not like we have a class to get to or anything."

We continue walking, but she doesn't let it go. "What just happened, Kat? It's like you saw a ghost or something."

I hesitate before answering. I don't want to say what I'm about to say, but I know it's the only chance I have of keeping Lucy safe. Everyone is in danger, and I'd never forgive myself if something happened to her that could have been prevented.

"There is something I have to tell you," I say, "and it's going to come as a shock."

"It's Roman, isn't it?" she says. "What is it? Is he gay? A transvestite? I always thought there something a little feminine about him—"

Despite myself, I laugh. "No, it's not about Roman," I say, aware that this is a bit of a lie, but Roman's vampirism isn't what's important right now. "It's about Lithia."

"What is it?"

"Well, I don't know exactly how to begin, but—"

"Oh, just spit it out, Kat."

"Do you believe in vampires?"

Lucy laughs. "Do I believe in *vampires?*" Then she sees that I'm not laughing with her. "Wait—you're serious?"

"I know it sounds crazy."

"Um, yeah. Crazy's a bit of an understatement, actually."

I realize she's less likely to believe me if I talk about vampires—that maybe I need to take a different approach.

"Halloween," I say. "I'm thinking of being a vampire."

"Oh." She looks relieved that her best friend isn't insane after all. "Well, why are you so serious about it? It sounds fun. Maybe we can be vampires together."

"Sure," I say. "We should definitely do something together. And speaking of togetherness, I've heard about a lot of bear sightings lately—"

"Really?" She wrinkles her nose. "I haven't heard anything about that."

"Cougars, too. You need to stay out of the park at night, and—well, just be heads up. Don't go anywhere alone. Ever."

"Really? I have to take Mercutio with me everywhere? Poor old me."

"I'm serious, Lucy."

She seems to hear something in my voice that makes her pay attention. We are nearing our classroom, and she stops, looking at me closely. "You're still thinking about Virginia, aren't you?"

Virginia was a fellow student; we all acted together in the college's production of *Measure for Measure*. She disappeared the night of the dress rehearsal, killed in the hills above Lithia. The police called it a bear attack, but I know better. It was Victor.

I nod. "I think about her a lot, actually."

Lucy's still studying me. "And you actually were serious about the vampires, weren't you?"

I nod again. It's always been hard to lie to Lucy.

"Vampires? In Lithia?"

"Yes," I say.

"And you're saying that a vampire is what killed Virginia? Not a bear?"

"Yes."

"How come I've never heard anything about this?"

"No one else knows."

"Well, how do *you* know, then?"

I sigh. "It's a really, really long story. You'll just have to trust me until I can explain. My point is—you have to be careful, Lucy. No one is safe right now."

She gives me another long, hard look, and I can tell she has a million questions that she can't ask because we need to get to class. "You sure you're not yanking my chain? Because if this is a joke, it's not all that funny."

"It's not a joke. I swear. I've never been more serious."

She studies my face. "Okay, Kat. I believe you."

I'm so relieved I give her a big hug. After losing Stacey, I never thought I'd be lucky enough to have another good friend. "Thank you for believing me," I say. "And please be alert. Even when you get distracted by Mercutio."

"What am I being alert for, exactly?" She looks around as if she might see a vampire walking past us on campus.

"That's what's so scary," I tell her. "They sneak up on you. Just don't spend any time alone—in the park, or the forest. Don't trust anyone or anything."

She looks a little doubtful, but she nods. "Okay. Now, I won't ask *why* there are vampires in Lithia, I won't ask whether you have a history of mental illness—I won't ask you anything. But I'll heed your advice."

"Thank you."

"Hey," she says, "if it means adopting Mercutio as my personal bodyguard, I'm all for it."

"Don't tell him I told you any of this."

"Don't worry," she says. "I don't want to see you in a straitjacket anytime soon." She sees my face and laughs. "Kidding! I won't say a word. Come on, we're late for class."

We hurry into the classroom and take our seats, and all the while I wonder whether I've possibly saved Lucy's life, or whether I've just made a terrible mistake.

———

"Did you feel it?" Professor Towson asks.

Nancy Towson is our geology professor. She's one of the youngest teachers I've ever had, and she bursts with enthusiasm for all things earth-related. I've never seen anyone so excited about the granite outcroppings above our valley.

"Feel what?" the girl behind me asks.

"The earthquake," Professor Towson says. "It registered a four-point-three on the Richter scale. Not too shabby."

"When did it happen?" I ask.

Professor Towson looks at her printout. "Four-fifteen this morning."

I sit up straighter when she says this. "How accurate is that reading?"

"Very. Though I have to admit," she adds with a smile, "that I slept right through it."

An earthquake, right at the moment of my nightmare. Was this a coincidence? I doubt it. Like Roman says, there are no coincidences.

And, on some larger scale, I doubt that my taking geology this semester is a coincidence either. I registered for the class after the recent earthquake that caved in the old Lost Mine—I wanted to learn more about the earth, about this region. And now, I wonder whether I am in this class for reasons I'm not even aware of yet.

Of course, my imagination is probably just running away with me. As Professor Towson told us early on, earthquakes are constantly happening, all around the planet. It's just that most of them are so small that we don't notice them. But the earth is always shaking, moving, breathing—just like people.

The quake last night wasn't strong enough to do any damage, but it makes me wonder again about what Roman and I were talking about—and about what Professor Lindquist had always spoken about: Gaia and the idea that the earth, when threatened, will protect itself.

I remember that Professor Towson told us last week that oil drilling has been proven to lead to earthquakes because it destabilizes the underlying earth. At what point does physics end and Gaia begin? Or are they one and the same?

Remembering the hot water up near the mine that day with

Roman, I raise my hand and ask, "Is Mount Lithia a volcano?"

"It is," Professor Towson replies, "though it's considered dormant. It last erupted about eight thousand years ago."

"Wow," I say. "A long time ago."

"A blink of an eye in geological years," she says with a smile. "But yes, it has been quiet since and still appears that way."

"So that earthquake wouldn't be related to the volcano?"

"That's the million-dollar question. Sometimes, yes, volcanic eruptions are preceded by earthquakes."

That's a scary thought. "How can we tell that's not happening right now?"

"We have monitors located at the top the mountain," she says. "And as of yet, we haven't detected any signs of volcanic activity. That's not to say that there isn't a connection. After all, it's the collision of tectonic plates that creates volcanoes."

Professor Towson goes to the chalkboard and draws, talking all the while. "We stand on a plate that is in conflict with another plate, with one being forced under the other. And as the plate moves further and further underground, it melts, and pressure builds—pressure that eventually results in a volcano."

"So you're saying it's just a matter of time before Mount Lithia erupts again?" somebody asks.

"Not at all," says Professor Towson. "It may never erupt again. The fact is, for all our scientific research, we know very little about how the earth works. But I'm not worried about Mount Lithia, or I probably wouldn't be standing here teaching you. I'd be far, far away!"

Professor Towson smiles again, and I feel a wave of relief. I guess I get a little paranoid when I don't get enough sleep.

After class, Lucy whispers, "Vampires and volcanoes and

earthquakes, oh my!" and I give her a playful punch in the arm. Then she and I part ways, and I grab an iced coffee at the student center and guzzle it down on my way to Lithia Runners.

Just before I enter the store, I look up at the mountain and wonder what secrets it holds. I finish the coffee and wish I'd gotten the next largest size; I really need to stay awake. After work, I've got homework and was hoping to go for a run. Instead, I call Roman and leave him a voice mail, asking if he wants to meet for dinner. I'm wondering whether he knows something about that mountain that Professor Towson doesn't. I believe her when she says that science doesn't have all the answers—and when it comes to Lithia, things are even more mysterious. Here, science comes into conflict with the otherworldly, and, too often, the otherworldly wins.

Ten

Roman isn't here yet, so I take a seat on the bench outside the restaurant. It's near Lithia Creek, and I watch the people go by. Seeing the tourists always makes me feel optimistic. Even though I see the dark side of this town—rather, the dark residents—most people have the time of their lives in Lithia.

When I see Roman I can tell something isn't quite right with him. For starters, he's smiling.

"What's funny?" I ask.

"Nothing."

"Then why are you smiling?"

"Am I?"

"Yes, you are. You never smile."

His smile actually widens when I say that. "Am I that much of a curmudgeon, Katherine?"

"Not really," I say. "It's just that you're always so serious."

"Perhaps I need to take life less seriously."

"But sometimes it is serious," I tell him. "Like everything

that's going on with Victor, and I have some questions about Mount Lithia—"

He comes in close and kisses me, which shuts me up pretty quickly and makes me forget what I was going to say. "Let's have a nice evening, Katherine," he whispers. "Let's not worry about the troubles of the world tonight."

I'm convinced. Roman's always had that power over me— to allow me to forget everything else that bothers me. When we're together, sometimes it feels as though the rest of the world disappears.

After dinner, he suggests a walk in the park.

"Aren't you worried about Victor?" I ask.

"I thought we weren't going to discuss Victor," he says.

"Right. I know. It's just hard not to, when I know he's lurking around."

"Don't worry," Roman says. "You're with me."

He pulls me close and kisses me for what feels like a nighttime, a lifetime, and again I forget everything—where I am, where we are, everything but the warmth of Roman's arms.

When he pulls away, he says, "I love you, Katherine," and I can see his eyes in the dark—nothing like Victor's eyes. Roman's are dark and bright at the same time, filled with hope and love.

"I love you, too," I say, and he smiles again. I could get used to this, seeing Roman's smile. If I thought he was gorgeous before, he's stunning when he smiles.

We walk along the creek. I feel a drop of water and look up to see sagging clouds above.

"It's raining again," I say.

Roman looks up but doesn't stop walking. "Do you want to go home?"

"No. I don't want tonight to end."

"Neither do I."

Rain keeps falling, but we keep walking, meandering along the trails, stopping to kiss every so often, continuing on—until finally we realize we're getting soaked. We hurry to take cover under an awning of the main theater building. Everything is dark and quiet.

"Come with me," Roman says, taking my hand.

I follow him to the back entrance of the theater. I remember another night when he snuck me into the theater and I tried on costumes for his upcoming Halloween party. It now seems like years ago that I was just getting to know Roman—it was before I knew what he was, who he was, and it was so far from who he is now.

"Do you believe in fate?" I ask.

We're in a dim hallway, and Roman's hand is firmly grasping mine. He's quiet for a minute, then says, "I used to fight it, Katherine. I didn't want to believe that it was my fate to become what I was—that I would be that way for the rest of eternity." He squeezes my hand. "But now—yes, Katherine, I think I would say I do. Because somehow I was brought to you, or you to me—and for that I'm very grateful."

We reach a row of doors, and Roman opens one and flips a light switch. It's a dressing room, and when I glimpse myself in the lighted mirror, I want to dive under the dressing table. My hair is stuck to my face, and I'd almost forgotten I was still wearing all black from rehearsal that morning—it has been such a whirlwind day that I never had the time to change.

"Wow, that's a scary sight," I say, staring at myself with embarrassment and a bit of horror.

In the mirror's reflection, I see Roman behind me, holding a towel. He gently dabs at my hair, then at my arms and shoulders.

"You should get out of those wet clothes," he says.

"Was this your plan all along?" I say, and in the mirror I can see him smiling.

He turns and opens a closet door. "Try this," he says, holding out an Elizabethan-era sleeping gown, like something Juliet would wear.

"Doesn't the costume department need this?"

"I'll have it laundered and back in this closet before they arrive in the morning."

As I slip it on, then slide off my wet things once the gown covers me, Roman, too, changes into a dry outfit. We are both looking at each other and pretending we aren't really looking. It would be too easy to get carried away.

Once we're changed, though, I look at him and feel a surge of electricity run through my body. Something about him in costume, and me in costume, about the two of us as Romeo and Juliet instead of Roman and Kat, is very seductive.

By the way he's looking at me, Roman seems to think so, too. "Come with me," he says, and I take his hand and follow him. Next thing I know, we are both on the stage. It's set for the balcony scene, and I run up the hidden stairs and emerge on the balcony, looking down on Roman. On Romeo.

I have spent many hours on the edges of this stage, watching a young Romeo feverishly in love with Juliet, who in turn is madly in love with him. Like Juliet, I lean over the balcony, and Roman gazes up at me, his body leaning toward me, like he'll begin to levitate at any moment.

I recite Juliet's lines as well as I can remember:

O Romeo, Romeo! wherefore art thou Romeo?
Deny thy father and refuse thy name;
Or, if thou wilt not, be but sworn my love,
And I'll no longer be a Capulet.

Roman stands below, smiling up at me—fully in character as my adoring Romeo. Or is he actually adoring Roman? Is that look on his face him in his role, or is it all for me?

I continue:

That which we call a rose
By any other name would smell as sweet ...

I forget the next line and skip ahead a little—glad right now that I don't have to memorize this part with everything else going on in my life:

Romeo, doff thy name,
And for that name, which is no part of thee,
Take all myself.

Roman moves closer, eyes on mine, and as Romeo he says:

I take thee at thy word.
Call me but love, and I'll be new baptis'd;
Henceforth I never will be Romeo.

Is it possible, I wonder, for us to ignore our differences, the way Juliet and Romeo thought they could? Can I forget I'm human and that Roman is not, the way Romeo and Juliet swore to forget where they themselves came from?

"Katherine."

"Sorry," I say. "I don't know Juliet's lines very well."

"Please," he says, "join me here." He steps backward and spreads his arms wide.

That didn't sound like Shakespeare. "Is this part of the scene?"

"No, Katherine. I'm asking *you*."

"Oh." I head down the narrow stairwell and onto the stage, where Roman is waiting. "What is it?" I ask.

"Right here," he says. "On this stage—this is where I first laid my eyes on you. Do you remember, Katherine?"

How could I forget? "Of course I do. I was in the fifth row. You were mesmerizing as Hamlet. I felt like you were looking right at me."

"I was."

I feel my face flush red, his eyes focused on me in that intensely Roman way.

"When I met you, my life changed forever," he says. "You changed me forever."

"For the better, I hope?"

"Of course. Before you, I never knew that I could be happy. That I could ever live a life of freedom from pain, from causing pain." He reaches out and touches my face. "It took the thought of losing you to make me realize I needed to change. You gave me that courage, Katherine."

"It's fate."

"I'm in love with you, Katherine. I feel as though I always have been, and I know I always will be."

I remember the first time I saw Roman, the way his eyes swept me right into his. "I think I've always loved you, too." I'm thinking back to how we began, drifted apart, came back together, and as my mind swirls with memories, I'm hardly noticing that Roman is kneeling on the stage in front of me.

"Did you drop something?" I ask.

I start to kneel down myself, but he stops me.

"Katherine," he says, "will you marry me?"

I can only stare at him, wondering if he's gone back to the play, whether he is suddenly Romeo again, not Roman. But I am quite certain that Romeo never uttered these lines.

He takes my hands in his and repeats his lines: "Katherine, my love. Will you marry me?"

Part Two:
Unsteady Ground

Eleven

Roman wants to marry me. Here he is, down on one knee, waiting for my answer. I need to give him an answer.

I love Roman with all my heart. But I never imagined being his wife. I am still getting used to being his girlfriend.

He is a vampire. How does this work? Something tells me that it's not going to be anything like the movies—nothing ever is.

"My dear Katherine," says Roman from the stage floor, "I am beginning to wonder whether your lack of response is your actual response."

Then he pulls out a small box and opens it to reveal a glittering ring—it looks a hundred years old, with intricate carvings in gold, studded with diamonds, one large diamond at its center.

I can't help but stare at it; I've never seen anything lovelier. "It's beautiful, Roman."

"It was once worn by a princess," he says. "And, once you put it on, it will be again."

He takes my hand to put on the ring, but I pull back.

"What is it, Katherine?"

"I love you, Roman," I say. "It's just so soon."

"If I've learned anything over all these years, it's that time cannot be wasted."

"I know—you're older than me, and wiser. But I'm still figuring it all out."

"What is it you need to figure out?" he asks.

"I'm not sure."

"You can take all the time you need," he says.

"Really?"

"I understand." He stands up and takes my hand again. "If you'd consider it, I'd love for you to wear this while you make up your mind."

He slips the ring on my finger, and it looks as though it was meant to be there. It fits perfectly.

"How'd you know?" I ask. "My ring size—how come this fits me so well?"

"Because you fit me so well, Katherine. We fit well together."

I look up at him. He doesn't look upset, or impatient—just loving and hopeful. "Hey," I say suddenly. "Is this the reason you saw David at the jeweler's? Because you were there buying this ring?"

Roman smiles. "I didn't buy that ring," he says. "I've had it forever, and until I met you, I didn't know if I would ever have a use for it. But yes, I did see David when I went in to have it sized."

"Clever man."

"The funny thing is," Roman says, "the jeweler didn't need to do anything. It was your size all along."

I look at the ring and realize Roman is right—time is a gift that shouldn't be wasted.

"If we are to marry," I say, "I want a long engagement. At least a year. I want to be able to drink champagne at my reception. Legally, I mean."

"As you wish."

"Marriage is forever, you know. It's not something you just rush into."

"I'm well acquainted with forever. I know what it feels like to live forever alone. And that's why I want to spend the rest of my days with you."

I look from the ring to his face, to the ring and back to his face—and then I'm leaping up, into his arms, and he catches me and hugs me tightly, spinning me around and setting me down just when I think I'm too dizzy to take any more. He sets me down gently on my feet and looks at me.

"Is that a yes, Katherine?"

"It's a yes. Yes, Roman, I'll marry you."

The kiss between us lasts longer than any kiss before, longer than any kiss in my life. We become one on that stage as minutes or hours pass—I don't even know. All I know is that I've now given myself over to him. Fully. Completely. Left bare my heart, knowing that he will not let it crash to the ground.

Twelve

I'm on the floor of Lithia Runners, surrounded by opened boxes and half-tied shoes, looking up at Mr. Ramsey. He's still coming in wearing the same old beat-up pair of running shoes. *It's all an act,* David says. David thinks Mr. Ramsey showrooms here, then buys the shoes online—but I don't get that feeling. I think that he just can't make up his mind.

I know the feeling. Despite my confidence in accepting Roman's proposal, I can't help but wonder if we're doing the right thing.

But I'm still wearing his ring, the glittery part twisted into my palm so it doesn't attract attention. I'm not sure I'm ready to announce the news, especially with David and Kendra's wedding coming up—but I also don't want to take off the ring, which Roman will surely notice.

"I think today is the day," I told Mr. Ramsey when he came into the store. David had pulled me aside and said, *Just tell him you're out of stock. Save yourself.*

But it's my last day in the store, and I want to close the sale.

David and Kendra are getting ready to be partners in work as well as in life, and business has been brisk enough to keep the two of them busy, but they don't truly need me on a regular basis anymore. And, I have to admit, because I'm getting ready to go to school in earnest, not just part-time, it's been hard to juggle this job as well as my theater work.

But change can be difficult. It's hard to imagine my life without Lithia Runners. My life as Roman's wife.

Still, if I've learned anything, it's that life doesn't give you what you expect. So maybe it's better not to think so much about it.

Mr. Ramsey asks to try on a new pair of trail shoes in two sizes. I sigh and head for the back room.

David chuckles as I pull boxes from the shelves. "You're never going to pull it off."

"I beg to differ," I tell him defiantly. All of a sudden, I want this more than anything.

"I haven't sold him a pair of shoes in years," David says. "That's all I'm saying."

"Ten bucks says I can do it."

Kendra walks in. "What's going on?"

David's eyes light up, and I wonder whether people notice this in me when I see Roman. I know what I feel like when he walks into a room—a flutter in my belly and a little jolt that feels like electricity—but does it show?

David explains our bet to Kendra, and she says, "Sorry, Kat, I'm with David. Toughest customer I've ever seen."

"Enough to put in another ten bucks?"

She laughs. "You're on."

Arms full of shoes, I make my way back to Mr. Ramsey. "Mr. Ramsey," I say as I lower the boxes to the floor. "Today you're going to buy a pair of running shoes."

"I hope you're right, young lady."

"I am right. Just wait and see."

I bring out the two pairs of shoes he asked for, as well as another I thought he'd like. I watch him work through each pair, stand and look at his feet in the mirror, mosey around the store, then sit back down and look up at me helplessly.

So I bring him three more pairs. Again, he circles the store. He sits back down and shakes his head. And so I grab three more. And try to be patient.

"Maybe it's not meant to be," he says as he tries on the last pair.

"I think today is your day," I tell him. "You know why?"

"Why?"

"Because today is my last day working here."

"Really?"

"That's right. And nobody knows your feet better than I do. Wouldn't you agree?"

"I guess so." He looks as though he's still trying to take in the fact that I'm leaving the store. "Where are you going?"

"I'm going back to school, full-time."

"Well, good for you," he says, and the genuine kindness in his voice makes me hopeful. Then he says, "These are lightweight, but a bit too snug on the toes."

"What about those?" I point to one of the other pairs.

"Too loose on the toes."

"And these?" I hold up another box.

"Low arches."

He says this with a resigned shrug. I can sense him getting ready to leave, so I sit next to him and look him in the eyes. "Mr. Ramsey," I say.

"Yes?"

"Sometimes you have to make decisions," I say. "They're not always easy. Like leaving this job—this isn't easy, not at all. This store has been my home for the past year. I'm still not sure if it's the right decision—but it's the best decision right now. And that's all I can go on, you know?"

At this point, I'm not even talking to him. I'm talking to myself, trying to convince myself that I'm doing the right thing. That I've got to think about my education. The land. Roman.

And all I can think of right now is that I will miss the smell of new shoes. I'll miss all of the bright colors, the nifty clothes and gear. And I'll even miss Mr. Ramsey.

He's getting ready to leave—he has stood up and is putting on his jacket.

"Well, maybe next time," I say, expecting him to turn and leave.

"Maybe now," he says. Then he bends down and picks up a pair of neon green shoes, the only ones he'd tried on twice today. "I'll take these."

"You will?" I feel as though this is a sign—a sign that I'm on the right track. If Mr. Ramsey can commit to a pair of shoes, I can do anything.

Plus, I'm twenty bucks richer.

I ring up Mr. Ramsey's new shoes and wave as he leaves the store. "You'll love them," I call out.

I'm standing near the window watching him walk down the street when I feel a tap on my shoulder. I look over to see Tyler Carlson—someone I haven't seen in a while. He was my acting buddy in *Measure for Measure*, Angelo to my Isabella. Though it's been a while, he looks exactly the same, with his cute smile, his baseball cap tight over his thick, messy hair.

"Hey, Kat," he says. "Long time."

"Yes," I say, not knowing exactly how to respond. Back during *Measure for Measure*, we were a bit more than fellow actors—but not for long. Tyler was a steady presence in my life, when I wasn't speaking to Roman and had broken up with Alex, and I still look at him and feel grateful for that. For the way he held my hand, for his constant optimism, which always raised my spirits. It also didn't hurt that he had striking eyes and a body that I loved to watch up onstage and in rehearsals.

"I never see you on campus anymore," he says.

"Oh, I'm still there," I say. "I'm still part-time."

"Ever going full-time? I don't want to be a senior before I see you again."

"Soon, I hope. This is my last day working here. But I'm a stagehand over at the theater, at least until *Romeo and Juliet* closes. I've been pretty busy, I guess."

I'm about to ask him how he's doing when a voice breaks in. "Are you two through socializing?"

I look over to see a familiar face—but not a very welcome one. I almost made it out of here without seeing her again. At least, until race day.

It's Erica. And it's clear by the way she's looking at me that not only does she recognize me this time but her rudeness is meant especially for me.

"What can I do for you, Erica?" I force a perky smile.

She gestures at the top row of shoes. "I need a size nine in all of them."

"All of them?"

"Of course." Apparently I hesitate for a moment too long because she continues, "You do work here, don't you?"

It's easy to remember why I so thoroughly enjoyed beating her at Cloudline. You'd think that her recent near-death experience on the trail might've humbled her a bit, but she's as dismissive, demeaning, and moody as ever.

I turn to Tyler. "I'm sorry," I say. "I have to get back to work. See you around?"

"Sure," he says. "Let's get coffee sometime."

"Sounds great."

I go into the back to get shoes, muttering under my breath as I stack the boxes high in my arms and return to the floor. Erica is seated in the middle chair like a queen waiting for her attendant.

"So, you running?" she asks, though it sounds more like a demand than a question.

I wonder if that's the only reason she came in—to find out. Maybe she's going to try on a hundred pairs of shoes, like Mr. Ramsey, without intending to buy anything.

I don't really want to give her the satisfaction of an answer. "Why do you care so much?"

"I like to know who's behind me."

"Really? Because last I remember, you were behind me."

She ignores this, leaning down to pull on a shoe. Then she tosses it aside without even standing up. "Are you sure these are size nine?"

"Positive. Maybe your feet have grown. Like your ego."

She eyes me as she pulls on another pair. "It's a pity you're a coward. I was looking forward to beating you."

She tries on eight pairs of shoes, and, as I suspected, doesn't buy a single pair. Even worse, she stands aside and watches me as I pick up the detritus of her little shopping adventure.

"Sorry," she says. "None of those were a good fit."

"It happens," I say, reminding myself to stay calm, that it's my last day here and I'll never have to wait on her again.

But as she leaves, I can't resist calling out, "I'll see you at the starting line."

She pauses as she reaches for the door, and I think I see a shadow of anxiety pass across her face—or maybe it's just annoyance.

I get back to cleaning up the mess. Kendra walks through the store and whistles. "Mr. Ramsey," she guesses.

"He's gone. With a new pair of shoes, by the way," I add. "No, this was someone even worse. Annoying Cloudline runner. Thinks she's God's gift to running."

"Oh, Erica."

"You know her?"

Kendra laughs. "Of course. She's second only to Mr. Ramsey in the ratio of number of shoes tried on versus number of shoes actually purchased."

"I was starting to take it personally. I beat her in Cloudline, and I think she's still upset about it."

"Well, here's hoping you do the same again this year," Kendra says. "Nothing would give us all greater pleasure."

"That's my plan, too. In fact," I say, "maybe I'll take the money you and David owe me and buy some sweet new shoes."

She rolls her eyes. "Cash or check?"

Thirteen

I look across at Roman, who's dressed in a suit. I am wearing a purple dress with an intricate flowery pattern woven through the skirt. The sounds of the creek flow beside us— the gentle rush of water, a few ducks splashing. A violinist is playing something by Vivaldi. There are about twenty attendees, in folding white chairs flanking a little path strewn with flower petals, watching as Kendra walks down the aisle with her father. Standing across from Roman, near the altar, I feel as though this could be our wedding. And maybe one day it will be.

Kendra wears a simple white dress, no train or anything frilly—just a simple, white cotton dress with flats. The dress fits her perfectly, and her hair is pulled back, with flowers braided through the strands. She looks almost like an angel gliding across the bed of pine needles that carpets the ground.

My thoughts are so jumbled right now—I'm thinking about Kendra and David and how happy I am for them, and I'm thinking about how I want to get married in a ceremony just like this one—and I'm also thinking about Doug.

Yesterday, I went to his office to see whether he'd been able to find enough serpentine and, if so, what kind of weapon he'd been able to make. The whole thing makes me very uneasy, mostly because I worry that Doug could have an assault rifle made of serpentine and it still wouldn't be enough—Victor is way too fast. And I worry we're being arrogant to think we can stop him ourselves.

But when I got to Doug's office, he wasn't there. The receptionist said that he'd planned to take a half-day off and that he'd be back in the afternoon. But when I returned, he still wasn't there. The receptionist didn't look too concerned, but I didn't think that was like Doug, to just take the whole day off without telling anyone. So I went back one more time before the office closed—still no Doug. The receptionist continued to shrug it off, saying he'd probably e-mailed but her e-mail was a little quirky that day. Still, I wasn't so sure.

Could Doug have dared to confront Victor on his own?

I knew he didn't want me to come along, but the two of us were supposed to work out a plan—together. Even if Doug had protested my involvement, at least I could have prepared him. Maybe I'd even have told Roman and Alex so he could have some backup.

What if he's missing—and it's all my fault?

I try to focus on the scene in front of me—the sun breaking through the pine trees, filtering them into a lighter shade of green. With the canopy of trees overhead, it's as if we're gathered together in a church filled with stained glass in all the colors of Lithia: greens and browns, golds and blues. I'm glad David and Kendra chose the church of nature, and of course these old-growth trees are far older and more historic than any of the local churches anyway.

I watch David as Kendra approaches, smiling at the happiness on his face. I feel as though Stacey is among us, somehow, and I know that she would be as happy for him as the rest of us are.

And there it is again—that nervous feeling. The thought of Stacey—and my role in her death, by leaving her on the trail as I raced ahead—reminds me of Doug and what I've gotten him into. I wish I could call him, but I don't even have his number; I always know just where to find him, at the parks department. He's always been so devoted to his job, to Lithia.

Roman catches my eye, and again I force myself to stop worrying. Roman looks as handsome as ever, and I try to imagine the two of us standing where David and Kendra are standing right now. Under an arch of flowers. Pledging our love forever. And, in the case of Roman, that's really saying something.

I wonder now how our marriage will be, with me being mortal and him living forever. Of course, I now know that it's possible for vampires to die—but they don't die like the rest of us, of old age, of natural causes. Roman won't die unless someone wants him to, unless someone wants him dead. Which is why Victor wants to kill me so badly—because he knows that eternal life without me would be worse for Roman than death.

And yet—many decades from now, I hope—Roman will have to face that fate anyway.

I've asked Roman if this sort of thing has ever happened, a human and a vampire getting married. He believes that it has, and he assures me that these couples have lived happily ever after—and yet he can't name them, or introduce me to them. I think maybe it's a vampire myth that he's carried with him all these years, a hope that he could someday find someone and be less alone in the world.

And children? I haven't even asked him about that. But I'm in no hurry. I think of Alex and his four dogs, and how he seems like a dad when he's with them, even though his "kids" have four legs instead of two—and I think I'll be happy starting with a few rescued dogs, or cats, or bunnies, and Roman and I can just see how it goes from there.

Basically, I need to worry less and focus more on the happy part of all this—in fact, I still have to get used to the idea of being engaged. So much of my life has been about running—from things and people and places. And now, my life is the complete opposite; it's all about staying put, facing down my demons instead of trying to outrun them. It's about staying in Lithia. I'm convinced now more than ever that this is where I belong.

I still need to figure out what I'm going to do with all that land—which I think ties me here to Lithia even more than Roman, or the theater, or David and Kendra, or anything else. The idea that I have something worth protecting.

Not only that—the opportunity to do good. I like Alex's idea of a nature center. Maybe I can go a step further—create a sanctuary for the animals that Alex seems to be collecting, maybe even before animal control gets concerned. He's working today, in fact—so dedicated to his new job that he couldn't take a day off for the wedding. I wish he were here, but it's easier this way, not having to look at him and feel awkward about being with Roman now.

"You may kiss the bride."

I realize I've missed the entire ceremony, but as I watch David and Kendra look into each other's eyes, I know I haven't missed a thing—in that one look are all the vows I didn't hear. Words couldn't have been more beautiful than the sight of them just now, turning around, hand in hand, to face us all as husband and wife.

I don't realize that I've let out a long, happy sigh until Roman says, "What is it, Katherine?"

"Oh, nothing," I say. "It's just so beautiful, isn't it?"

"Yes, it is."

"Not to be a copycat," I say, "but I want to get married right here."

"As you wish," he says, and kisses me.

The reception is held a few feet from the creek at a row of picnic tables dressed up in tablecloths and lanterns. In a small clearing people dance to romantic, classical music, and Roman whisks me onto the "dance floor"—nothing more than dirt and pine needles, which is the best dance floor I can imagine. I'm not sure what I'm doing, but Roman is a wonderful dancer, and I let him take the lead.

"I am already imagining our wedding," I whisper to him.

"Really?" He sounds pleased. "I must admit, Katherine, when I proposed to you, I wasn't certain I would get the answer I was hoping for."

"I didn't mean to be hesitant," I say. "Not at all. It's just— something I haven't thought about yet. I'm still so young."

"Am I too old for you?"

"Only by about a century or so."

Roman laughs. He was twenty-six when he died, which means he is twenty-six forever.

Our moment is interrupted by Kendra calling my name. When I turn toward her, she waves me over.

"I'm tossing my bouquet," she says. "I want you to have a fighting chance."

I suppose, even though I'm engaged, it can only be a good omen if I catch her bouquet. Besides, the flowers are gorgeous, and I wouldn't mind having them in my cottage.

Kendra turns her back to us and heaves the flowers high into the air. When I see them above me, I surprise myself by leaping into the air to catch them.

Kendra cheers, and a moment later Roman comes over. "So, you're the next to get married, Katherine?" he says, right in front of everyone.

"We'll see about that," I say. We haven't told anyone about our engagement, and no one has looked at my hand and noticed the ring. This is one of those secrets that's fun to keep. At least for now.

The two little flower girls are looking longingly at my bouquet, and I bend down and hand it over to them. "It looks as though there's enough flowers here for each of you to have a mini-bouquet," I tell them. "Think you can do that?"

They nod eagerly, and the next thing I know they're sitting at the edge of the "dance floor," pulling apart the flowers and putting them in each other's hair. I hope Kendra doesn't mind.

Suddenly, the sound of thunder erupts in the sky, and I look up. I haven't seen any lightning, and until now, this has been the clearest, most perfect day. Oddly, despite the thunder, I still can't see a cloud in the sky.

Then I realize what it is—all at once, I feel as though I'm standing on a boat on the high seas—only it's the ground itself, moving beneath me in a slow, wavy, but unmistakable motion.

An earthquake.

I hear a shriek and look over to the tables in time to see the plates and glasses tipping, some of them falling onto the ground. People are holding on to the tables or each other, and the motion abruptly goes from a slow, rolling motion to a fast, jerky one.

It happens so fast I don't even know it's over until I realize I'm sitting on the ground, along with many others, all of us wide-eyed and not quite sure how we got there. Dead tree branches are falling, and I catch a faint smell of smoke, not like a fireplace but something different—a dark scent, like oil burning, or tires. Something black and hot.

Just as I try to stand up, the shaking begins again, and it's even more violent this time, like water beginning to boil. The trees sway so hard above us it's as if they're being driven by a fierce wind—though there's no wind at all—and I begin to worry a giant ponderosa pine could topple onto us.

I reach my arms out to catch myself when I fall again—but Roman's next to me, holding me up, and somehow he is staying on his feet.

And then it stops, just like that. I straighten up, still clinging to Roman, and look around. Most of the wedding guests are on all fours, just beginning to get up, or they're clinging to one another, to the trees, to the picnic tables, which have now been stripped of their food and decorations. I hear the sound of a child crying—it's one of the flower girls, and Kendra's beautiful bouquet is now scattered everywhere.

As everyone gets up and dusts off, it becomes clear that no one is hurt. The wedding reception site is a mess, but no trees have toppled, and nothing is damaged other than the lovely food and decorations—including the beautiful, white-frosted vegan wedding cake.

Everyone's clothing is also a bit of a mess, and I see Kendra trying to get a big smudge off her wedding dress. But she doesn't linger at it very long, and then David jokes, "This marriage is already off to a shaky start." Kendra gives him a playful punch in the arm for that, and he pretends to be gravely injured.

With that, the music begins again, and David and Kendra get the dancing started. I realize that Roman has disappeared, so I pitch in with a few others doing cleanup. After a few minutes, the tables are covered again, and we manage to save some of the food that hadn't yet been uncovered.

Even as the party continues, there's a sort of anxiety in the air—if nothing else it's just the knowledge that something awful could have happened here, on this special day. There's not enough food left for everyone, and I'm hoping that people don't decide to leave early—I don't want anything to spoil this for David and Kendra.

Roman reappears, and I go up to him. "May I have this dance, Katherine?" he asks.

"Actually," I say, "I was wondering if there's something we can do about the food situation. And a couple of wine bottles broke, too. I want everyone to stay and have a good time."

"It's already taken care of," he says, and smiles.

"You mean—"

"I placed a call," he says. "The Lithia Food Co-Op is sending someone over immediately with all the vegan food they have onsite, as well as their special vegan cupcakes and a few extra bottles of champagne."

I throw my arms around him. "You're a hero, Roman. I made a good choice when I said yes."

We go to the forested dance floor and join the happy couple and the others who are beginning to dance. The day has been salvaged—yet I still have a nagging feeling about Doug. I am hoping he hasn't done anything as foolish as go into the hills alone—and that if he did, he wasn't anywhere near anything that could have fallen on him during the earthquake.

Fourteen

Romeo and Juliet has begun previews, which means the show hasn't "officially" opened but is performed live to an audience, and a bit of tinkering still remains.

With Roman back at the theater, the productions are selling out quickly. As a stagehand, I get a good view of the audience between acts, and during this afternoon's matinee, I can tell the audience is loving the show. Or maybe it's Roman they love—I also notice that most of the audience consists of young women.

I still haven't found the time to reach Doug—with an all-day rehearsal and homework yesterday, and the matinee today, I haven't had a free moment to get over to the parks department.

Another weird thing I've noticed is that despite the wedding "jitters" in the park, there were no reports of earthquakes anywhere in the news. I'm glad I have geology class tomorrow— maybe Professor Towson will be able to tell me what's going on. With her access to all that special equipment, she can at least tell me what it measured on the Richter scale. I expected it to be big enough to warrant a little news coverage, at least.

I remember what David had said—a shaky start. He meant it to be funny, of course, but something tells me it's actually quite serious, only I'm not sure exactly why.

After the performance, I wait around to see both Lucy and Roman before I head over to the parks department. Neither of them know what I've got cooking with Doug, and I want to keep it that way. So I'm trying to figure out some sort of excuse for not hanging around and celebrating with everyone.

I see Lucy and wave. When she comes over, I give her a big hug. "You were amazing," I tell her.

"You think? I felt like I was mumbling all my lines."

"You sounded fine."

"Stan thought I was too frenetic, kept moving out of my light."

"Given what almost happened to me, how can he blame you for that?"

She grins. "So you're waiting for the boyfriend, I presume." Then she grabs my left hand. "Love the ring, girlfriend," she says. "Who knew you were into fairy-tale bling?"

"Well, actually … " I watch her face look at mine, suspiciously.

"What are you saying, Kat?" she says. "That this ring is *real?*"

I nod.

"You and Roman? Are you kidding me?"

"He asked last week."

"And you waited until *now* to tell me? I hate you."

"I still don't fully believe it myself," I say. "I guess I just needed to get used to the idea."

"I hope you didn't make *him* wait that long."

"No," I say. "Only about five or ten minutes."

She gives me a look. "So, tell me—how'd he do it? Fancy

restaurant? Hot-air-balloon ride?"

"Right over there on the stage. We snuck in after hours."

"Nice. Did he get on his knees?"

"Of course. He's Roman."

"Good," she says. "If they don't get on their knees *before* you marry, you can forget about that posture after you get married."

"You're such a romantic," I say. Then I ask her what I've been asking myself for days. "Lucy, am I too young for this?"

"Well, let's just say this is one time you can be glad you don't have parents. If I came home with an engagement ring they'd both have heart attacks, then they'd lock me up somewhere until I was thirty."

I don't say anything—I'm thinking, for the first time, about how my parents might have reacted. My father, of course, would have found a way to profit from it—pawning my ring, getting me into some wedding-planning scheme. But I think my mother would have been happy for me. She'd caution me to take my time, but she'd tell me to follow my heart. Sort of what I've been thinking all along. This makes me feel happy—the feeling that maybe I've turned out to be a lot like her.

"Hello? You there, Kat?"

"Yeah, sorry."

"Anyway, you don't have to answer to anybody, so who cares as long as you're happy? Besides, you're an old soul, and he's an older guy. What is he, like, thirty?"

"He's twenty-six." Give or take a hundred years or so—but I can't tell Lucy that. She was open-minded about learning Lithia has vampires—but that might change if she learns I plan to marry one of them.

And ignorance, as they say, is bliss—she's smiling. "I'd say you two are going to live happily ever after."

"I hope you're right."

"I'm always right," she says.

"Do you mind keeping this a secret for now?"

"Me? I love to keep secrets."

"No, you don't."

"Yeah, I guess you're right. I love to *divulge* secrets. But I'll do my best with yours, even though you and Roman are the worst-kept secret in Lithia."

"Thanks."

"Now, are you going to ask me?"

"Ask you what?"

"To be your maid of honor."

"I have to ask? I'm just waiting for you to start planning the shower and get bossy about what color your dress should be."

"Very funny."

"We're just going to have a small ceremony," I say. "And it may be years from now."

"I don't care when it is," Lucy says. "A chance to dress up and meet a hot groomsman? I'll be there."

I see Roman across the room; he's looking at me and nodding at something someone else is saying. He looks as if he's ready to leave but can't quite get away.

"There he is," I say. "Looks like he needs rescuing."

"I'll get him," she says. "I'll tell him you need to see him about that sword prop in the first act."

Moments later, Roman is at my side, and he's as eager to leave the theater as I am. As we walk down the street, I tell him about Lucy's enthusiasm for our engagement. "She's going to be my maid of honor," I say. "Now, what about you? Who's going to be your best man?"

Roman sighs. "I'm afraid I don't have any family to speak of."

"You have David."

Roman considers the idea. "I'll ask him tomorrow."

"Too late," I say. "David and Kendra are on their honeymoon already. They left for Hawaii this morning."

"And they left you all alone in charge of the store?"

"They closed the store for the week. There's a big sign on the front door that says JUST MARRIED. I did offer to fill in, but David said it would've been tough to manage on my own. He also said, and I quote: *Life is short.*"

"Well spoken."

"Except for you," I say. "You're going to live forever."

Roman takes hold of my hand. "Nothing is forever. Not even me."

He has gone very serious, and we walk silently down the street, hand in hand. He's right. Nothing is forever.

Which reminds me that, as much as I'd like to spend the afternoon with Roman, I need to get to the parks department.

"Roman, I have to go," I say. "Maybe you can rest awhile, and we can have dinner later?"

"Where are you going?"

"To—to see a friend."

"Why don't I come with you?" he says.

"No," I say. "I mean, that's okay. You must be tired from the performance."

Roman looks at me, as if he knows there's something I'm not telling him. "Secrets between a man and his wife already?"

He's right—it's not fair to keep things from him, especially something like this. And the fact is, I could need Roman, especially if Doug has gotten himself into trouble. So I relent and tell him that Doug knows there's a vampire in Lithia, a dangerous one. "He doesn't know his name," I say. "And of course, I didn't tell him about you. Or Alex."

Roman frowns. "I told you, Katherine, this is not a game."

"I know that," I say. "But Doug is the only one—the only human, or mortal, or whatever—who I can talk to. And I wanted to get his advice. Human advice." I tell him about Doug's plan and I watch Roman's face darken. "We need to do *something*."

"No. *I* need to do something. You and Doug—or the entire parks department, for that matter—are no match for Victor."

"But what about his plan? You have to admit it's a good idea. That it could work?"

"It's possible, I suppose," Roman admits, "but you're still playing a deadly game, Katherine. I will come with you."

I shake my head. "The Lithia Theater Company's most famous actor showing up at the parks department all nosy about one of their employees? You'll draw too much attention to Doug. I already am myself, just by going back there looking for him. I'll keep you posted, I promise. Go take a nap at my cottage. I'll be there as soon as I talk to Doug."

"That's it? Talk to Doug and return to me?"

"Yes," I say, though I know I'm not being totally honest. That if Doug is up in those hills somewhere, I'm going to go looking for him, with or without Roman. Hopefully with.

"I'll be waiting for you."

We part ways, and as I hurry over to the parks department, I find myself hoping that Doug is finally there to talk to.

Fifteen

I stand outside the office for a moment to catch my breath, since I don't want to be the crazy person who keeps bursting into the office asking where Doug is. I open the door and approach the reception desk.

"Hi," I say. "I'm wondering if I could speak with Doug Gibson?"

The receptionist looks at me. "And you are?"

I hesitate for a second. She's never asked me this before when I've come looking for Doug. "Kat Healy."

"And what is this regarding?"

"It's—a park issue I talked to him about—a couple weeks ago. I'm just, um, following up." I'm pretty sure I sound like a lunatic, but I'm not prepared to answer questions.

"I can take your name and number and have someone call you."

"Is something wrong? I mean, shouldn't he be in the office today?"

"I can't comment on his schedule."

I step closer to the desk. "Look, I actually had an appointment with him last week, and I'm a little concerned about why he didn't show up. Is there anything you can tell me?"

She gives me a suspicious look.

"I'm just worried, that's all. It's so unlike him."

"I know it is." The woman glances around, then says in a quiet voice, "We haven't heard from Doug in several days, and we're looking into it."

"What? What happened? When was he last seen?"

She looks around again, putting her finger to her lips. "I'm not supposed to talk about this," she whispers. "I don't know anything other than the police are involved and we hope they find out where he is."

"What can I do?"

"Nothing," she says. "Don't tell anyone what I've told you. I'll have him call you as soon as he's back."

I nod. I say, "Thank you." I don't acknowledge what I sense we are both thinking: What if Doug doesn't come back?

I run back to my cottage, where Roman is waiting. I put on my running shoes and tell him we're next going to his place to get his. "We're going for a run," I tell him.

"Must we, Katherine?" he says. "A nap was the original plan, wasn't it?"

"The plan's changed."

"You still have plenty of time to train for Cloudline," he says.

"This isn't a training run," I tell him. "We're going to look for Doug."

"Katherine ... " he begins, disapprovingly.

"Roman, we can either go get your running shoes and go up the trail together, or I can leave right now and do it myself. But either way, I'm going up there to see if I can find Doug. He's been missing for days."

"All right, Katherine."

Fifteen minutes later, we're running up the Lost Mine Trail. I'm still in only moderately decent shape, but I'm fueled right now by worry, and fear—and the horrible feeling that if anything's happened to Doug, it will be all my fault.

We make it almost all the way to the top, but we haven't seen Doug anywhere, and finally I have to take a break.

"Where could he be?" I wonder aloud, leaning down and resting my hands on my knees, suddenly completely exhausted.

"What do you think happened, Katherine?"

"I think he made the serpentine blade and tried to find Victor himself. And if he found him—" I can't bring myself to finish the sentence.

Roman looks serious. "If he and Victor did meet, that does not bode well for Doug."

"I know that." Then I begin to feel a bit of hope. "Unless—I mean, do you think that blade could have worked?"

Roman shakes his head. "Not unless Doug knew what he was dealing with, and it sounds as if he didn't. He sounds as stubborn and foolish as you, Katherine."

"And he's as protective as you," I say. "That's why he came up here without waiting for me—he knew I wanted to come along and didn't want to put me in danger." I take a long, deep breath. "The irony is, I could've helped. He might've had a chance."

"Or you could both have perished," Roman says.

I look up toward the hills. "Let's go to the top. See if we can find anything."

"You know that you are not likely to find him on the trail. Victor wouldn't be so careless."

"We still might find a clue or something. Or maybe we'll find nothing. Maybe I'm just overreacting. Maybe he just took off for a wild weekend away or something."

"Perhaps you're right," Roman says, but he doesn't sound any more convinced than I am.

We jog up to the top of the trail, and I see nothing along the way. Scanning the treetops, I begin to feel hopeful—maybe I let my imagination get away from me. Maybe I'm worrying over nothing.

"Come on," I say to Roman, "let's head down."

We've had a vigorous run, and we start down the hill at a brisk walk. Despite my new hopeful outlook, I'm still glancing down at the trail, looking for broken branches, signs of a scuffle, anything that might offer a clue.

Suddenly I stop in my tracks, and I feel Roman directly behind me. "What is it, Katherine?"

"Look." I point toward a piece of rock in the bushes, near the edge of the trail. A piece of serpentine.

Roman bends down and picks it up. He holds it out to me, and I look at it in the palm of his hand. "It's not just a rock," I say. "It's been carved." My hand instinctively goes to my neck, but my necklace is still there.

"It's a fragment of something larger," Roman says, taking a closer look.

"A blade?"

"Perhaps."

I look around, then call out for Doug. Then again, louder.

No answer.

"Katherine, if this is what you think it is, I'm sorry to say that Doug is not going to answer."

"We need to keep looking for him," I say, starting into the woods from the place where Roman had picked up the serpentine.

Roman grabs my arm. "You aren't going to find him."

I begin fighting Roman's grip, trying to pull away, until he releases me and I fall into the leaves. And then I see it. Tiny drops of blood scattered across the leaves. "Oh, no."

Roman kneels down next to me. "I'm so sorry, Katherine."

"This is all my fault," I say. "I got him involved in this."

Roman shakes his head. "From what you told me, he was already involved. And you specifically told him to talk to you before making a plan. It's not your fault he decided to act on his own."

I straighten up. "We still need to go find him."

"Katherine, don't you see?" Roman says. "We'll never find him—unless Victor wants us to. He's not like the others."

"What do you mean?"

"Remember your friend Virginia? Her body was found because Victor wanted her to be found. He was sending a message."

"So why do you think Doug is different?"

"Because Victor knows you've gotten the message," Roman says. "And what Victor needs now, more than anything, is to build up his troops."

"I don't understand."

"What I'm saying, Katherine, is that Doug is one of them now. He's been recruited, and if Victor gets his way, he'll use Doug to lure in more victims."

"You mean—"

Roman nods. "If you do see Doug again, do not talk to him. Do not go anywhere with him. Keep your necklace with you and don't be afraid to use it. You need to be very careful."

"I *am* careful, Roman. Always. What I'm worried about is the rest of Lithia—all the people who don't know. All the people who trust Doug. None of them are safe now, are they?"

"No," Roman says, "they're not."

"We have to warn them."

"How, Katherine?" Roman says.

I feel my energy deflate. "I don't know."

"We will stop him," Roman says. "If it's the last thing I do, I promise you, Victor will be stopped."

We continue back to town in silence, and as the horror of the day weighs down on me, I am hoping this is a promise Roman will be able to keep.

Sixteen

I'm not exactly sure what caused that earthquake the other day," says Professor Towson.

She's standing in front of a huge map of Oregon and California. The maps illustrate the underlying plates, fault lines, and volcanoes. I see Mount Lassen down in California and Mount Hood up north of Portland. Professor Towson points to various lines as she offers various explanations but then raises her arms in the air. "It's a mystery."

"Why?" I ask.

"If this were a standard earthquake, we'd have a reading that correlated with one of the fault lines. Yet the source of the earthquake was Mount Lithia."

"So it's a volcano?"

"I don't know. Mount Lithia has been dormant for thousands of years. There's no sign of a pending eruption. We have monitored this mountain in the past and detected no activity whatsoever."

I look at the door, waiting for Lucy to barge in late, as she often does. She is the only one missing from class today. Normally we are short a few students, but with the earthquake, Professor Towson's class is one hot ticket.

"Now, with this latest temblor," Professor Towson says, "we'll be looking into it further, of course. But it's still quite unlikely that this little shake means the volcano will erupt again anytime soon—if ever."

I don't want to worry about Lucy, but recent events have shaken my confidence that anyone is truly safe in Lithia. And after what happened to Doug, I'm all the more terrified at the thought of something happening to Lucy.

I'm beginning to wonder if perhaps Victor has already won. How many more friends do I have to lose before it's over? Maybe it really is for the best that I leave Lithia. At least that will save the few people I still do have left.

I'm grateful that David and Kendra are on their honeymoon—at least I don't have to worry about them. But eventually, they'll return, and if Victor's still here—well, something's got to give.

I try to focus on the rest of the class, but I can't concentrate. I hear Professor Towson say she's going to spend time on the mountain with other experts and all their monitors, and that they will wait to see if the ground shakes again. It's not a comforting thought—that some of the smartest people in town have no idea what's going on—and yet I shouldn't be surprised. What's been happening in Lithia for hundreds of years isn't exactly explainable, least of all by science. Vampires, ghosts, necklaces with strange powers—who'd believe it?

Awakening volcanoes—that's a new one, and I hope Professor Towson is right that the little quake doesn't really mean anything. Lithia has been through enough lately.

When I walk out of the classroom, I hope to see Lucy in the hall, or on the quad, or in the little juice bar where she's been spending a lot of her time. It's not unlike her to skip a class now and then, and not at all unusual for her to be late—but her not being around at all makes me anxious. Maybe this is actually Victor's grand plan—to make me go insane. If it is, I think it's starting to work.

Outside, I sit down on a concrete bench on the edge of the quad and send Lucy a text. I hear rapid footsteps, and when I look up, I see Tyler running toward me. He looks terrible—his face is pale, despite the fact that he's been running, and he looks alarmed. Like he's seen a ghost—or worse.

I stand up to meet him. "Tyler, are you okay?"

"Come quick," he says. "It's Lucy."

"What is it?"

"Follow me, Kat. I'll take you to her."

"Where?" I ask. "What happened?"

But Tyler has already started off, and I do my best to keep up. I've almost forgotten what a good athlete he is, and right now he's even faster than I remembered. And this makes me even more worried—I always set new personal records when I'm running out of fear, and Tyler seems to be running on the same fuel. I'm wondering where Lucy could be, whether Tyler has called the police, whether I should call Roman. But I don't have time to ask these questions or even to think—Tyler's moving too quickly, and I'm doing all I can to keep up.

Then I realize that Tyler is headed for the Lost Mine Trail.

And my body begins to slow with dread.

"Tyler!" I call out. "Slow down!" I'm yelling as loudly as I can—at this pace, anyway—but Tyler doesn't hear me. Or maybe he's running too fast to answer.

My legs are burning, as well as my lungs, but I keep Tyler in sight as we enter the trail and the sun becomes blocked by the trees. I welcome the burst of cool air and wonder how much farther into the woods Tyler is going to lead me.

He turns off the trail, and I shout at him again—in vain. It's impossible to run this fast now that we're off the trail; I have to leap over tree trunks and branches, through bushes and fallen leaves. I feel the sharp edges tearing at my clothing and the skin under it—and just when I think I can't go any farther, Tyler stops in a clearing just ahead.

"Where is she?" I ask, gasping for breath.

I get another reminder that I'm not ready for Cloudline: Unlike me, Tyler doesn't seem winded at all. But something else is wrong—he's looking around as if he's lost.

"Are we in the right place?"

His head swivels around, his body following, until he does a full circle.

"Tyler, answer me. Where's Lucy?"

Tyler turns until he's got his back to me, and I begin to realize that something isn't right here. Tyler isn't winded. He isn't breathing heavily. His body is still and calm, as if we haven't just run at full speed two miles into the hills.

I begin to back up.

He turns around, and that's when I see his eyes, glowing red, and the fangs overhanging his bottom lip.

"Lucy won't be joining us," he says.

I keep backing up, slowly. I think I can feel my necklace against my neck, but I don't want to draw attention to it by reaching for it. "Tyler," I say, "what happened to you?"

Tyler steps toward me, and I counter with two steps back.

"Did Victor do this to you?"

Tyler doesn't answer. He just keeps coming forward, determined, and I keep backing up, trying not to fall over all the broken tree limbs.

"It *was* Victor, wasn't it?" I say, hoping to stall him. "Tyler, tell me. What happened to Lucy?"

I don't know whether it's working; he is still moving slowly. But the ravenous look in his eyes hasn't changed—maybe he's just savoring the anticipation of killing me.

"You don't have to do this," I say.

"I don't have a choice," he says.

Finally I reach up to make sure my necklace is still there— thankfully, it is. Tyler doesn't seem to notice the gesture at all. Apparently, if Victor did send Tyler up here to kill me, he didn't warn Tyler what he had to reckon with first.

"Everyone has a choice," I say. "Roman changed. So did Alex. You can, too."

And then Tyler lunges at me, and I brace myself for the flash of lightning. The light bursts against my eyelids, and then I hear a hideous scream and smell the pungent odor of smoke.

I open my eyes to see Tyler on the ground, his hands over his mouth. It's over. I've won—for the time being.

I lean over him, my necklace dangling over his weakened body. "Where's Victor?" I ask. "Did he send you here to do this?"

"He was supposed to be here. To help." Only now does Tyler seem winded, unable to catch his breath.

"Where's Lucy?"

"I don't know."

I don't want to touch him at all, but I put a foot against his cheek, and he groans. "Tell me!"

"I don't know. Honestly."

I lift my foot and turn to go. But after taking a couple steps, I turn back. "I meant what I said," I tell him. "You don't have to do this."

"What are you talking about?" he manages to say.

"You can survive off of trees and plants. It's a lot easier than what you're doing now. And obviously a lot better for everyone."

I can't tell whether Tyler is listening; he seems to be in a lot of pain. My necklace must've dealt a stunning blow for a new vampire—but on the other hand, maybe these newly created vampires are the most open to change.

I help Tyler to his feet. "Tell Victor his days are numbered," I say. "No, better yet. Stay away from Victor. Find Roman, or Alex. They'll help you."

Tyler looks at me, still stunned. I'm not sure he's heard or understood me, but I've done all I can do. I turn to go once again—I need to find Lucy, and I have a feeling I'm going to need some help.

—w—

First, I go to the theater. The show's not for a few hours yet, but I'm hoping that Lucy has arrived extra early; she often does that to "get in the zone," as she says with her usual flair for the dramatic.

But when I get there, all the dressing rooms are empty, and only a few crew members are around, getting the set ready for the production.

Exhausted, I sit down in one of the house seats to check my phone. Lucy hasn't texted me back, and this is what has me most worried. Lucy lives on her phone, in a constant state of buzzing and ringing and texting.

I try calling, but it rings and rings and rings, and my heart sinks when I hear her programmed message. I leave a hurried message, telling her to come to the theater immediately. Then I hang up and I call Roman. No answer—but that's no surprise. Roman still has trouble with new technology and rarely answers his phone.

I take a deep breath and try to calm down. I know if I wait patiently, in all likelihood, Lucy will show up in another hour or two, as she normally does. But normal doesn't mean anything anymore—especially not here in Lithia. There's no such thing as normal these days.

I can't shake the thought that she might not show up at all. Or that Victor got to her just as he got to Tyler. Maybe she'll show up, but in a different form, ready to lure an unsuspecting cast mate into a dark corner.

I go out to the courtyard and watch the people milling about. The scene out here is picture-perfect; no one would ever suspect the darkness that lurks around them. Both tourists and locals are gathering, already excited about the evening's show. Getting ready for dinner beforehand, enjoying the crisp fall weather. Window shopping. Holding hands. Oblivious to the dangers all around us. I envy their blissful ignorance.

I catch a glimpse of someone who looks just like Lucy; I start toward her, then save myself from an embarrassing encounter at the last minute. I start walking around, into the gift shop, down to Main Street. I pop into cafés and sandwich shops, one after another. I walk around peering into store windows until I realize I'm in the Pioneer District, not far from Roman's house.

I pick up my pace until I reach his front door. I knock but get no answer. He'd given me a key, but I don't have it with me. I pull on the door in frustration, surprised when it opens.

I walk in and call his name. No answer. He's not there— probably out for a run. At least Roman's one person I don't have to worry about.

I stand in his sparsely furnished living room and look out the window, wondering where Lucy could be.

"Katherine?"

I look up to see Roman standing in the doorway.

"I didn't know you were here."

"I just got home," he says. "Is everything all right?"

"Lucy's missing."

He looks puzzled. "No, she isn't."

"Yes, she is. I've been looking everywhere for her."

"Katherine, I just saw Lucy. She's fine."

"What are you talking about?"

"I dropped her off at the theater a few moments ago."

"I was just there. Like, half an hour ago." I throw my hands up in the air. "Do you know how worried I've been?"

He comes over and puts his arms around me. "What happened?"

I tell him about Tyler, how he used Lucy to lure me into the hills.

"Are you all right?" He holds me at arm's length and studies me, as if to make sure there are no body parts missing.

"I'm fine, Roman. The point is, Victor's getting more dangerous by the minute. And Lucy—" I shudder, thinking of what could've happened. "I'm so glad she's okay."

"She is absolutely fine, Katherine."

"We need to warn her about Victor."

"Not necessary."

"What? Don't you realize that she could—"

"What I mean, Katherine," Roman gently interrupts, "is that she already knows."

"You told her?"

"No," he says, "she told me."

I turn away from him and sit down on the sofa. "Now I'm really confused. What are you talking about?"

"She came here," Roman says. "She said she was on her way to class and noticed someone following her. When she described him, it was clear to me that it could be no one but Victor. She went to the theater, hoping you would be there, and when she couldn't find you, she stayed on the main streets until she got here."

"So you told her who he really is? I mean—*what* he really is?"

"I didn't want to," Roman says, "but then she told me that you'd already said there are vampires in Lithia. She suspected, and I simply confirmed she was correct."

"I did," I confess. "I had to warn her. I didn't mention him specifically—and, of course, I didn't mention you or Alex. But I had to tell her there are vampires here in Lithia. She needs to know, to stay safe."

"People shouldn't know about us, Katherine. It's dangerous."

"Dangerous? For who? Lucy would be dead now if I hadn't said something."

"I understand, but—"

"Roman," I say, standing up. "I think it's time we started opening up. People need to know the truth."

"We cannot send the whole town into a panic, Katherine, and you know that."

"But we have to stop Victor," I say. "I can't live with myself knowing that he's finding more victims."

"I know. But I must be the one to do it. Do you understand?"

"Do what, exactly?"

"I don't know. All I do know is that from this point forward you should trust no one. You need to protect yourself."

"I know that already."

"As you saw today, Victor will go after those closest to you because he knows they can get closer to you than he can."

Again I'm relieved that David and Kendra are far away from here. And that my parents are no longer on this earth to fall victim. I'm better off alone, now more than ever.

Suddenly the truth of what Roman is telling me gives me a terrible thought. "Can I trust *you*?"

"Always."

"But how do I know that? You just said—"

"My dear Katherine, Victor has done all he can do to me in one lifetime. You can trust me." He pauses, then continues. "And, as much as it pains me to say it, you may also trust Alex. This I know."

"Okay." I look at him for a long moment, but he says nothing more. "So, what's the plan?"

"We can't rush it, Katherine. Give me some time. Victor has been around too long. This won't be easy. You must be patient."

"I can't," I say. "Roman, you've been dead for too long to know how precious life is. I can't let this continue."

I open the door.

"Katherine, where are you going?"

"I'm going to give Victor what he wants. Me."

Roman follows me to the porch. "Please, Katherine. Don't be impulsive."

"I can't live like this, not anymore. David and Kendra are going to return to Lithia in a week, and then what? Kendra will be first on Victor's list, and you know that. He's going to go after everyone I care about until there's no one left. And it's my fault. I'm the common denominator here, and I can't take it anymore."

Roman pulls me close, and I collapse into his arms. "It's not your fault, Katherine. I was just like Victor once, and I can tell you this for certain. We are made to kill. It would happen with or without you."

"Victor's different. He's evil."

"I agree. He will never change. And we need to stop him. But we can't do it if we don't plan carefully. Look what happened to your friend Doug."

"Don't remind me, please, Roman."

"Then I'll remind you of another, very important thing," he says. "Which is the fact that I can't survive without you."

I have become his greatest weakness, his vulnerability. And I understand.

"Tell me what to do, then," I say.

"Give me time. Just a few days. I need a plan. But I promise you I will come up with one, and I will take care of Victor. Alone."

"Not alone," I say. "There's someone else you need."

Seventeen

Until Roman comes up with a plan, I've decided to avoid people. I've called in sick at the theater. At school. I've called Lucy and told her not to go anywhere alone, ever. And I've spent all day up on the land, my serpentine necklace securely around my neck.

Something about this land is so peaceful. I feel almost as though nothing can harm me here—as if I don't even need the serpentine. Not that I'll ever test that theory.

I'm beginning to make noticeable progress on clearing away the mess from the fires. The piles of debris have been hauled away—two Dumpsters' worth, loaded by me and Alex and hauled away by the trash company. Most of the wood will be recycled, so at least all these trees did not die completely in vain.

Mostly, I'm trying to stay busy to keep my mind off of Victor. I promised Roman that I'd give him time, but time weighs heavily on my shoulders.

When my muscles are aching too much to continue, I take

a break and sit on one of the concrete foundations, the biggest one, surveying the valley below me. What a view this would've been from the house that was supposed to be here. I can see the entire town of Lithia below, the rooftops of the houses peeking out amid the green, the curve of downtown, the interstate, and then the rolling hills beyond.

I hear Alex before I see him—or, rather, I hear his pack of rescues. I watch for them, see them emerge from the road, Alex being towed by his pack of dogs. They're all panting, tongues lolling, and one of them gives me a hello bark.

Alex pulls a couple of portable water bowls out of his backpack and fills them. As the dogs take a drink, he comes over and looks around.

"Looking great," he says, surveying the land.

"How's Lucy?"

"She's good," Alex says. "She told me to tell you she misses you. And to get back soon because she doesn't like that other stagehand."

I laugh. Because I can't get close to Lucy without putting her in danger, I've asked Alex as well as Roman to keep an eye on her. "When you see her again, tell her I definitely hope I'll be back again soon."

"I will."

"So," I ask, "how's it going?"

I've not only asked Alex and Roman to keep watch over Lucy—but I talked them into putting their heads together to find a way to stop Victor.

"Alex?" I prod. "Do you two have a plan for Victor?"

Alex pauses before answering. "We're working on it."

"Ah. I have a feeling that means no."

"It means *not yet*," he says. "I know the waiting is difficult. But you know Victor as well as we do. He's not easy to surprise. And he's strong. And getting stronger."

"Why do you say that?"

"I don't know—Roman says he can sense it. He thinks Victor is planning something."

"Well, we already know that."

"No, I think Roman means something bigger."

"Then I hope you two come up with something fast."

"We will." Alex turns away from me and takes in the view. "I'm going to miss this."

"What are you talking about?"

He sits next to me. "I think I'm going to leave, Kat."

"Leave Lithia, you mean?" I can't believe what I'm hearing. "Why?"

"For one, I got evicted. My landlord got too many complaints about the dogs. I was never supposed to have pets there anyway."

"Oh."

"So much for that security deposit. But the trouble is, I can't find another rental in this town, not at my budget and not with my brood of mutts."

"I have money, Alex. I can help."

"I don't want charity, but thanks. I need to find a place to live that I can afford. And if it's not meant to be Lithia, I'm going to have to live with that."

"No. I refuse to accept this. I don't want you to leave."

"Kat—"

"No. Listen to me. You can stay at my place."

"I don't think Roman will be very happy about that."

"Roman and I—" I stop, not sure how to continue.

But Alex already knows. "Kat, I can see that ring from a mile away. I know you and Roman will be living under one roof eventually. But I can't ask you to rush anything on my account." He looks out over the landscape again. "Maybe it's best that I move on."

"But why?"

"Why do you think? This hasn't been easy on me, you know."

His eyes tell me what he's trying not to say. Seeing me and Roman together. Hand in hand. Knowing that we're getting married. And now, he's working side-by-side with the man he most resents, all for the greater good of keeping me and Roman together, forever.

"I'm sorry," I say.

"Don't be. I had my chance, and I blew it."

"You didn't blow it. It wasn't meant to be, that's all."

"Well, you're not going to convince me of that."

"Alex, you were my first friend here, my *best* friend, and in fact, you still are. I can't imagine Lithia without you. Please don't leave. At least consider staying. I'll even share dog-rearing responsibilities with you."

He smiles, but it's a sad smile. Then he shakes his head. "Speaking as another guy, I don't think Roman would like the idea of you and me raising dogs together."

"Roman knows I have a past with you, and he'll have to accept that we will always be friends."

"But maybe I don't want to accept that you will always be with Roman."

I can't think of anything to say. I've never imagined Alex would leave Lithia—he belongs here, even more than I do. Even though I haven't spent a lot of time with him lately, I can't imagine not being able to see him anytime I want, as selfish as that is.

And then it hits me. "Stay here."

"Stay where?"

"Here. On my land. I mean, it'll be a while before it's anything more than a campsite, but it's been approved for utilities already. We can build out one of these foundations right away and make a little cabin." I stand up. "This one, in fact. I think it has the best views."

"With what money, Kat?"

"Alex, you know that I have enough money to take care of the land, and then some. I can't think of anything better to do with it."

"Than to spend it on my housing expenses?"

"No," I say. "To build a cabin for the caretaker of my animal sanctuary."

He looks at me. "What are you talking about?"

Even I didn't know what I was talking about until I said it just now—but I realize that this is what I've dreamed of all along. "Can't you see, Alex? This is a perfect spot for a sanctuary. And you're obviously already running one, with all those dogs you've got."

"It's a brilliant idea, Kat," he says. "I'm just not sure—"

"I don't care what Roman says, and I don't care about the money, and I don't want to hear you say no again. Come on, Alex—you have to admit, it's the perfect solution." I watch him think about it. "And you know the dogs would love it."

"Would they ever." Alex stands up and paces around in a circle, eyeing the land with a new vision. "Okay. I'll think about it. I have until the end of the month before I get kicked out. Let's see how it goes with Victor first."

"Well, I'm going to find out who can build out this foundation.

Something simple—a lobby and offices downstairs, caretaker quarters upstairs. A big fence for, say, about four dogs. For now."

Alex is smiling, and it's a much happier smile than the one of a few moments ago. "Don't get ahead of yourself, Kat."

"I'm not. I've got to get this done before winter sets in, either way. And this sanctuary *will* need a caretaker—someone who's good with animals and has a bit of veterinary training. If that happens to be you, great. If not, I'll just put out a job listing."

He laughs. "I'll take that under advisement." Then he gathers his dogs, and I watch them disappear down the road.

Eighteen

I don't hear from Roman or Alex again until the next day, when Roman comes over before that day's matinee at the theater. He's limping, and when I demand an explanation, he admits that he and Alex tried to capture Victor in the woods—but Victor fought back and then outran them both. Alex suffered a few cuts to his face, and Roman twisted his knee.

"How are you supposed to do the show this afternoon?" I ask him. "Romeo is a young kid, and right now you're gimping around like an eighty-year-old man."

"Don't worry," he says. "I'll be fine. And don't worry about Victor, either. We'll take care of him."

But I do worry. This was supposed to be over by now, and I'm having a hard time believing anymore that they can do it. Victor is too strong and, with each failed attack, Roman and Alex seem to be getting weaker, as if Victor is sapping their strength with each encounter.

I've already decided to go to work at the theater this afternoon, but I don't tell Roman because I want to stop somewhere else first.

I wait for him to leave, then I walk across town to my mom's grave. It's been a long time since I last visited.

When I get there, I see that the rock I had left on the headstone has fallen, probably from rain or wind. I put it back up.

I begin to talk to her as I always have. "Do you think I have the courage to face Victor? I know I have the necklace—but what does this mean exactly?"

I think for a moment, gazing at the cool stone of my mother's grave.

"Does this mean that *I'm* the one who is destined to kill Victor?" I ask. "That I must succeed where Roman and Alex have failed?"

I am asking these questions of a headstone, and I look around to make sure I'm alone. I know I must look like a crazy person, but it's such a comfort to talk to her, even if she can't respond.

"Am I doing the right thing, marrying Roman?" I am thinking of the news that Alex might be leaving Lithia, how that shook me. I love Alex—but am I still in love with him?

"Can you really love just one person forever?"

I think about the animal sanctuary, how I'd never have thought of Roman for that—only Alex came to mind. Is he a closer soul mate to me than Roman will be?

I try to shake the doubts from my head.

"Can one person ever really make a difference?" I ask. "Can I build this sanctuary and make it work?"

I feel as though she is responding to me—not in words, but I feel a swell of positive energy about the sanctuary, about the ideas that are now swirling inside my head ... a place for animals ... for outreach ... for education. A place where kids can come to play and learn from their fellow creatures. A place where they can learn to treat the planet well.

A place where the good will outweigh the bad in this world.

But for this to happen, Victor must be stopped. And he will be stopped—even if it means I must be the one to do it.

———

Lucy is in the dressing room, makeup done, when I find her at the theater. There are only a handful of people around, but I drag her out of the dressing room and down the hall anyway.

"You're back," she says. "Does this mean all's well?"

"No," I say, "but I got tired of hiding out. And I wanted to see you. I haven't seen you since—" I find myself unable to finish the sentence.

"I'm okay, Kat," she says. "I know you're worried, but I can take care of myself."

"No one's safe right now," I say.

"That's what I'm saying. I went and got Roman, remember? I'm not going to do anything stupid. Not when I have this brilliant acting career ahead of me."

I grin. "So true."

She leans close and whispers, "Not to mention another date with Mercutio. Talk about something to live for."

"When this is all over, we'll have to go out together. A double date."

"Kit-Kat, I'm blown away. You actually know what a double date is. *And* you want to go on one."

"I've got to get to know the guy my best friend is falling for, don't I? And he *does* have a real name, by the way."

She shrugs. "We're Mercutio and Nurse. Works for us."

"Oh, you just like playing doctor."

She laughs, then gets serious a moment later. "So—Roman's like Victor, isn't he?"

I pause. I know Roman wants to keep this a secret, but I can't lie to Lucy. I lean in. "He used to be like Victor," I say. "But he doesn't hurt people anymore."

She looks confused. "Then he must be mighty hungry."

I explain to Lucy, as quietly as I can, everything about Roman. I include Alex as well, while I'm at it. I might as well come clean—and it feels good to have my best friend in on this secret at last.

"And you were the one who converted Roman?" Lucy asks.

I nod.

"Well done, Kit-Kat. Soon the whole world will be plant-based."

I smile. After hanging out with me for so long, Lucy has given up almost all animal products. I never actually talked her into it—she's always been addicted to that juice bar—but the more she learned about animals, the more she realized she couldn't be a part of their suffering.

"Lucy, I need a favor."

"What's that?"

"After today's show," I say, "I need you to cover for me."

"How so, exactly?"

"Roman will be expecting to see us both home, but I've got a few things to do. Alone."

She narrows her eyes at me. "Like what?"

As much as I hate keeping secrets from either of them, these are extraordinary circumstances. "Wedding stuff," I tell her.

She laughs. "You? Seriously? You haven't even set a date."

"I know, I know. I just have a couple of errands. And I need to do these things alone."

Lucy looks doubtful. "I don't know, Kat. It doesn't seem like a good time to be out there running around by yourself. Can't these errands wait?"

"No," I say, "they can't."

She purses her lips at me.

"It's the middle of the day," I point out. "And I'll be in public the whole time." Mostly, I add silently.

Lucy finally agrees. "Fine, but you text me as soon as you're home safe and sound."

"I will."

"Promise?"

"Promise."

Nineteen

As soon as the performance is over, I sneak out the side door of the theater. I wasn't lying to Lucy, exactly— I really do have a couple of very important errands.

They're just not all as safe as I promised.

But the first one is. I stop at the offices of Michael Stover, Esq. I don't have an appointment, but his receptionist knows me and lets me in. I sit down across from him and tell him I need him to prepare my will.

He looks stunned, as you might expect when a twenty-year-old comes in asking about a will.

"It's just a precaution," I tell him. "I want to make sure my land is protected. That it is used as I intended."

"This is highly unusual, Kat," he says.

"I know. But it's important to me."

He sighs and pulls out a notebook. I outline my plan for the sanctuary. We go over my options, and he tells me he will draw up the paperwork.

"How soon?"

"What's the rush?"

"No reason," I tell him. "I'm just eager to get started and want to make sure everything's in place."

He nods. "I'll have the paperwork drawn up tomorrow. I'll give you a call when everything's ready, and you can come in and sign."

"Thanks, Mike."

My next stop is the office of an architectural firm in town that is known for green design and building. I go in and ask for an appointment with the owners. The receptionist looks surprised to see a young face before her, asking for the next available appointment with the best-known builders in town. But when I say, "It's for the Horton property," she gets me on the schedule right away.

And then I'm on my way to my final errand.

This errand takes me out of town a bit. I head up the hill but not toward the trails, the woods. Instead, I turn right. Toward the castle.

It's then that I realize my errands have taken me a bit longer than I'd planned, and it's already getting dark. The sky is clear, but the moon is just a sliver above. The good news is that in this near darkness, no one can see me or where I'm headed.

Victor's house.

I know what I'm about to do is stupid. Suicidal. I know this, yet I feel compelled to do it. I've had enough.

At the front door, I try the handle and am not surprised the door is unlocked. Why would a vampire need to lock his door? It's quite the opposite—Victor welcomes anyone foolish enough to enter of their own volition.

And here I am, doing exactly what he wants.

The entryway is dark and dusty, and I wonder if anyone has been living in this place, if Victor is even still here. I reach for a light switch on the wall—I find one, but it doesn't respond; there's no light, no electricity.

"Victor!" I yell, my voice echoing throughout the house.

I walk down the main hallway, glancing into the many rooms—a dining room, a parlor, a ballroom. I keep looking all around, just to be sure he isn't lurking somewhere behind me.

Upstairs, I move from room to room. Even up here, there is a darkness that seems to overpower what little light makes it through the dusty windows. I see the room that I once spent the night in—long ago, when Roman used to live here, the night Roman brought me home after I tried to run away from Lithia. It's the same, museum-like space—white walls with ancient-looking oil portraits on the walls and a bed, now layered in dust. It looks exactly the same except that there is no hint of life at all.

I wonder where Victor's bedroom could be—is it possible that I might catch him asleep? If he does sleep. I just don't know what to believe about vampires anymore. Roman says that, contrary to myth, they don't sleep in coffins during the day to avoid the light, though they do prefer the darkness. And of course, sleep is not something an undead person ever needs anyway, though Roman will close his eyes and go into a meditative state at times. He says it's restorative. If only I could get by without sleep.

I see no sign of Victor upstairs, so I make my way down another staircase and find myself in a large library. I didn't even know there was a library here—this house is absolutely endless.

At the far end of the library, the streetlight causes a glint of something on the wall—a large knife mounted near the fireplace. This is no Swiss Army knife, I realize as I get closer; it's easily a foot long and slightly curved, with a handle made of cherrywood. If I'm going to protect myself I might need something more than a necklace—so I grab the knife. It's heavier than I expected and has intricate carvings alongside the blade.

I leave the room, holding the knife close to my body, trying not to slice off a piece of my leg with it as I walk. I head down another hallway, beginning to feel very lost because I no longer have any idea whether I'm in the front of the house or the rear. I'm starting to feel jumpy and keep looking left and right, spinning around, knife ready, thinking that this would be the perfect moment for Victor to pounce.

But the only sounds I hear are my breathing.

I feel a burst of heat, and I stop. Slowly, I turn toward it. Ahead of me is an open doorway, and beyond the door frame is a set of stairs heading down. I strain my ears and hear what I think is a furnace, though it could be my breathing. This is definitely not a place I want to explore, but I know I have to. I'm not doing this to walk away without getting what I came for.

"Victor!" I yell down the stairs. I hear no response, no sounds of movement. I stand in the doorway for another long moment, feeling the heat, hearing the breathing of something—or someone—down there. I hope it's only a furnace and nothing more sinister than that.

I can't do it. I can't go down there.

I back away and continue down the hallway. Then I hear it. A voice? A whisper? I can't be sure, but it sounded like my name.

And it was coming up from those stairs.

I take a deep breath. I don't know if it's the hot air coming from downstairs or the fact that I'm terrified, but I'm sweating, the heat engulfing me.

"Okay, fine," I say aloud. "Come out, come out, wherever you are."

I pass through the doorway and begin a slow, steady walk down the stairs. I'm oddly comforted by the heat—usually when Victor is near, I feel a sudden burst of cold air, like Erica had that day on the trail.

But if the chill means Victor is nearby, what does this oppressive pocket of heat mean? What sort of ungodly creature could be down here?

At the bottom of the stairs, I feel as if I've entered another world. Gone are the paneled rooms, the museum-quality art, the perfect layout of every piece of antique furniture. Ahead of me is what appears to be the entrance to a cave.

A cave? Inside a house? I strain my eyes to see as far ahead into the entrance as possible, but I see only darkness. Maybe this is Victor's creative idea of a wine cellar.

I must be crazy to consider going inside. Yet I am walking toward the entrance as if I have no other choice in the matter, as if I'm not moving on my own but am being pulled by some other force outside me. I don't even know if I could turn and run out of the house if I wanted to—and what good would it do if I did? It would only delay the inevitable confrontation between me and Victor. I've accepted that no matter what, it has to happen; it's the only thing he wants.

And if it happens sooner than later, he can't take any more innocent lives.

I leave behind the smooth, polished travertine floors for the jagged edges of the cave. I continue slowly, allowing my eyes to adjust to the darkness. I always thought caves were cold and damp—but the air in here is hotter than ever. The walls of the cave are dark and hard to see, but when I reach out and touch them, they are rough and moist from humidity.

I take a few more steps in and realize that I can see where I'm going—that it's not entirely pitch-black in here but that there is some sort of dim light source ahead. I have no choice but to head in that direction.

How far have I ventured into this cave—twenty yards? Thirty? It's hard to keep track when you're tip-toeing forward and trying to breathe air that feels like an underwater sauna. But eventually I leave the narrow passageway and enter what looks like a waiting room, hand-carved out of dark stone. There are dim, flickering lights on the rock walls, and I'm facing not one but three narrow entrances—to the left, right, and straight ahead.

I feel as though I'm on some grim game show where I have to choose between door number one, door number two, or door number three—except that on the other side is not a prize but the choice of how my life will end.

How am I supposed to make such a decision?

I try to think of which path my mom would choose. I'm wearing her necklace and, knowing this, I feel I have a fighting chance down here. The odds may be steep, but thanks to this necklace, I have powers of my own at hand, maybe even enough to force Victor to leave Lithia for good.

She would continue straight ahead, I think. My mother rarely backed down, and she rarely veered off course. She didn't doubt herself but made a choice and believed in it. And I know that if she were in my place right now, she would keep walking straight ahead, right into that middle passage.

So I do the same. I don't know how much farther I need to go, but I'm determined to see this journey to the end.

I see a flicker of light ahead and pick up the pace—despite my fears, I also want to get it over with. I'm now so deep into the cave, so deep into this passageway, I begin to worry about how I'll ever get out.

Or maybe that's the point. Maybe I'm not meant to leave here again.

The heat is now becoming unbearable, as if I'm heading straight into a giant cauldron. I hold out the knife in front of me and turn the corner just ahead.

I stop and look around, stunned. I have entered a towering cathedral of stone. I crane my neck, looking up at a ceiling studded with sharp, glistening stalactites. All around me, like hands reaching up, are stalagmites, many taller than I am. I walk around them gingerly, as if they are museum sculptures. I don't know why, but I'm heading to the far side of the room—again, as if I'm being drawn there, the wall flashing oranges and reds, the sounds of the furnace rising up.

Yet as I get closer, I see that the source of the heat is not a furnace but an open pit of fire, glowing around the edges.

I walk tentatively to the edge and look down, and that's when my head goes dizzy and I have to back away for fear of falling in.

A moment later, when I recover, I peer over the edge once again, to make sure I actually saw what I think I saw. I am looking down, hundreds of feet into the earth, at a lake of molten lava. Waves of red and orange molten fire are exploding and falling onto themselves, smoke rising up in pale fumes and disappearing before they reach my nose.

Again I step back, trying to catch my breath; the heat has sapped it away.

"Welcome."

I don't need to turn around to know it's him. I take my time, getting a firmer grip on the knife with my sweaty hand, taking a second to make sure my necklace is in place. Then I turn to face him. He's standing far enough away for me to point the knife at him.

"I believe that knife belongs to me," he says.

"Does it?" I ask. "Are you sure it doesn't belong to any of your other victims? You seem to have quite a collection of treasures in this place."

"Does it matter where it came from?" he says. "All that matters is that it is now mine. Not yours."

"Why don't you come get it, then?"

He laughs. "My, my, Katherine. What on earth has come over you?"

"You should know, Victor. You seem to know everything."

"All I know is that you have broken into my home and appropriated a family heirloom."

"I came here to convince you to stop."

"Stop what?" His face stretches into a ghastly smirk.

"Stop killing people."

"Oh, that. Can you blame me, Katherine? You take Alex away from me. Then you take Roman. I have to replenish the stock."

"I didn't take them from you. They left. And if you were smart, you'd join them."

"Me? Drink the blood of trees instead of people? Oh, please." Victor's face is as pale as ever despite the heat. "I am far too set in my ways to change now. Besides, I have a tradition to uphold."

"Calling it tradition doesn't make it right."

"Traditions are how we honor our ancestors. Traditions bind us. Traditions ennoble us."

"Some traditions, sure. But what you're doing is violence—plain and simple."

"And yet," he says, "you aim a knife at me."

"I don't want to hurt you. I just want you to stop hurting others."

Suddenly I feel the earth drop out from under me, and just as I'm trying to find my footing again, it catches me again—and then, another release, another catch.

Before I know what's happened, I'm on my knees, trying in vain to stand up. Another earthquake? I'm wondering. And then, much more important right now than figuring out what the movement was, I wonder what happened to the knife I was holding.

I straighten up to see it under Victor's left foot.

"You should be careful when handling a knife, my dear," Victor says. "You could have gravely, even fatally, injured yourself."

I look up at him. "Did you just do that?" I ask.

"Do what?"

I don't bother trying to snatch the knife back. He is much closer now, and I notice that I have very little room—I am trapped between Victor, an arm's length in front of me, and the fire pit, just a half step behind.

"Did you make the earth move like that?"

"Do you understand where you are, young lady?"

"All I know is we're in some sort of cave," I say.

"It's so much more than a cave, my dear Katherine. The fire behind you—do you know what fuels it?"

I shake my head.

"That, my dear, is magma," Victor says. "Liquid rock. We are standing in the heart of Mount Lithia, the white-hot beating heart. Magma pumps through its veins, keeps it alive. This magma, unleashed, is destruction incarnate. And creation."

"I'm in the heart of a volcano?"

"Should the pot boil over, then, yes, a volcano it would be."

"Do you—do you control it?"

"Control? You mortals are obsessed with control. You like to believe you can control the earth. But you are naïve. Nobody controls the earth."

Victor takes a step closer to me. "There are, however, ways of coaxing the earth into doing what you wish," he says. "I don't consider it control so much as cooperation. These tunnels. Your boyfriend helped build them, you know. Some were for gold, but some of the tunnels serve other purposes—like the tunnel that brought you here."

"I thought you hated fire."

"Is that what Roman told you? Of course. Because you are trying to rid the world of *me*. Searching for the elusive heel of Achilles. Well, you are correct. I dislike fire—but I also draw power from it. One of the many ironies of life. That which we fear also gives us power. Katherine, you, too, could have this power."

"I don't need it."

"You say that because you do not believe you can be any more powerful than you already are." Victor gives me an intense look. "But that necklace of yours has given you a taste of power. The serpentine around your neck—it was born right here. This mountain holds many special powers, and they can be yours if you only will embrace them."

"How? By becoming like you?"

Watching his face, I realize I'm right—he's trying to convert me. I'm hoping to make a vegan out of him, and he's hoping to make a vampire out of me—by choice, not by force.

But even though the idea repulses me, I also realize that he'll only let me have choice as an option for so long before he moves on to force. So I'm hoping maybe I can buy time by pretending to be interested.

"Is that why you haven't killed me yet?" I ask. "You'd prefer to make me one of you?"

"Of course," he says. "Not just one of many, but one above all others. You are special, my dear. I should have seen it all along, the power you exerted over Alex and Roman. But now I am certain of it. You are special indeed."

Despite myself, I'm intrigued. "I don't understand."

"Don't you see? What mere mortal would have dared enter this chamber? What ordinary human would have mustered up the courage to come face-to-face with me? There is a fire within you, a fire as strong as the vein of magma below us. That fire, Katherine, pulses with so much energy that if you could only learn to harness it, you could rule the world."

"Alongside you, of course."

"Of course. But what a power couple we would make, my dear."

"I'm sorry, Victor, but I'm already taken. Or didn't you hear?"

"Hear what?"

"Roman and I getting married."

"Is that right?" His voice remains calm, but I can tell I've surprised him. I watch his eyes erupt into the color of the fire behind me.

"Yes, that's right. Roman and I are going to be the next power couple, not you and me. Not you and anyone."

His eyes flash a bright red. "Then allow me to kiss the bride."

Victor steps forward, but I am already running—darting around the sharp stalagmites, using them as shields as he lunges for me. He could capture me in a fraction of a second if he wanted—this I know for certain—but what he's doing is trying to find a way to snatch my necklace. To make me vulnerable.

I see the exit ahead of me, and I rush for it. I'm almost there, and I'm actually starting to think I'll make it, when he appears in front of it.

"What's the hurry? You have an engagement party to attend?"

I find myself backing up again. Victor is no longer smiling. His expression is blank and empty, his eyes glowing like embers.

I know now that I can't escape this cavern. I have to take a stand now and fight—it's the only choice I've got.

I plant my feet and glance behind me. The ledge to the boiling cauldron of magma is still a body's length back, so at least I have a bit of room to back up if I need to.

We face each other, and I wait for him to make a move. When he doesn't, I grab my necklace and hold it up to remind Victor of what he must go through if he wants to get to me.

Yet Victor doesn't seem bothered in the slightest.

"That bauble won't stop me from killing you," he says. "I offered you life eternal, and instead you cling to happily ever after."

He picks up the knife and tosses it high into the air, and I watch it twirling and twirling down until he catches it without looking. "I don't even need this knife to finish the task."

I feel fear prickling my body from the inside out. My only hope is that he may be bluffing, that he's trying to get me to surrender the necklace by claiming it won't protect me. He steps toward me, and I step back. I can feel the heat from the fire pit searing the back of my legs, and I glance behind me to make sure I'm not too close.

Then the room rumbles, and the ground under me gives way. Another earthquake—and I hear the molten earth boiling and feel the heat of it coming closer as my feet shift under me, my body falling, falling, falling.

Part Three:
Last Rites

Twenty

I'm clinging to the wall, a few feet below the ledge. My feet are burning with the closeness of the fire. My fingers are hot with pain. I can't hold on much longer.

Victor is staring down at me. He shakes his head.

"It's a pity you will die from natural causes. I would have liked to play a more active role."

I say nothing, focused on concentrating all my energy into my fingers, each one lined up, one after the other, each playing a small but important role in saving my life, in keeping me here and not down there.

I won't be able to hold on forever, and every second that passes takes me further away from climbing my way back up. The heat and gravity are working in tandem, wilting me, sapping what strength I have left, tugging at me, willing me down.

Somehow, though I was prepared to do this, though I came here prepared to die, I refuse to believe this is it. I refuse to let go.

But as much as I want to hold on, I can only control my body for so long; there's only so much I can demand of it. I feel myself slipping and cling tighter, the pain in my hands nearly unbearable. I feel a shake, and my left hand slips free, my arm waving wildly. I hear someone scream and realize it's my own voice. I reach blindly up, and my hand finds another place to grab. Even through my panic and pain, I can tell that it's a foot lower than before, my hands uneven now.

I'm moving in reverse. Making my way down, not up.

Victor. Not only does he want to kill me—he wants to enjoy it.

"Oops," Victor says.

I raise my head. He's wearing an evil smile, his head cocked to one side, as if he's genuinely interested in watching me expire as gruesomely as possible. The thought of him taking pleasure in this enrages me, and I grip even tighter.

Then he extends a hand.

"This is your last chance, Katherine. An invitation to life immortal, to power without limit. Join me—before it is too late."

Then I hear a voice, shouting Victor's name—this time, it's not my own.

It's a man's voice, and it seems to surprise Victor even more than it surprises me. He turns his head toward the sound.

"Down here!" I shout. "I'm down here!"

Then Victor is gone—he disappears so quickly I don't know what happened, and I try to turn my head to look for him without losing my tenuous grip on these hot rocks.

I want to shout again but don't know if I have the strength. Gathering a breath, I look around again, but I see only the cavern's ceiling above. Then, before I can call out again, I hear voices, then loud cracks, like baseball bats slamming into rocks. I hear screams, growling, otherworldly sounds. I can feel the impact of bodies onto the earth, reverberations in my fingers and body. Another scream.

It has to be Roman—who else could it be? But what if he's unsuccessful again, and what if the consequences are more deadly than his last encounter with Victor?

This may be my only chance to climb out, while Victor's distracted. I need to get up there. I let go with my lower left hand and try to will it higher, but I find that I have no energy left, and I can barely move. Now loose, my left hand is flailing as it seeks a resting place. My eyes are blurry with dirt and sweat. I want to cry out once more, but I can't. I have no more strength.

Don't let go, I tell myself. Do not let go. But my right hand is now so overburdened and strained it doesn't even feel like my hand anymore—it feels like nothing more than an extension of me that I helplessly watch as it clings to a rock. A hand that is slowly, inevitably weakening.

I close my eyes. I can't bear to watch as it fails. As it lets go.

I feel it give—and yet, at that moment, when I have nothing left holding me up, I realize that I'm not falling. Something else is holding me, pulling me up. I open my eyes, and I see arms, bringing me to safety.

Then I see Alex's face, close to mine. A moment later, my feet are on solid ground.

"Are you okay?" Alex asks.

It takes me a few seconds even to start wondering how Alex got here and where Victor is right now. Because I'm focused on being alive. And I'm focused on Alex's arms, still holding me. Focused on the fact that I'm clinging to him as if I'll never let go.

"Kat?" Alex pulls back and lifts my face until I'm looking him in the eye. "Say something."

I'm so grateful, so relieved, all I want to do is curl back into Alex's arms. Maybe forever.

I hear another voice from within the cave, and it brings me to my senses. I pull away from Alex, as if I've been snapped back into reality. Which I suppose I have.

"I'm fine," I say to Alex—and to Roman, who has just entered the cauldron room. "I'm fine," I repeat. "Where's Victor?"

"He's gone," says Alex.

I look at Roman. He looks relieved, but not happy. He has a long cut across his left cheek, and his clothing is torn. Then I notice that Alex's clothing is also torn and burned.

"What are you doing here?" Roman asks.

"Trying to finish what I started. How did you find me?"

"Lucy cannot keep a secret," Roman says. "She knew you were up to something, and you should feel very fortunate to have a good friend with a big mouth. Otherwise, you would not be standing here right now."

"Did you kill him?" I ask, but Roman, still angry, doesn't answer. I turn to Alex. "Did you?" My hopes rise at the slightest possibility of Victor's demise.

Alex shakes his head. "Unfortunately, no. We cornered him, but he got away."

"What are you doing here, Katherine?" Roman asks again. There is an anger in his voice I haven't heard before—my Roman, always so calm, is furious. "Are you trying to kill yourself?" he demands.

"No—of course not. But I've told you—both of you—I'm not going to stand around while Victor preys on my friends."

Alex looks uncomfortable, and I don't blame him, having to witness this little domestic scene. "Look, I'm grateful you're here—I can't even express how grateful I am," I say. "But I really felt I had no choice."

Roman comes to me and takes my face in his hands. "Katherine," he says, "if we hadn't gotten here when we did—"

"I know," I say. And now I'm the one who's uncomfortable, knowing that Alex is now witnessing the making-up portion of our argument. "I'm just tired of running from him, you know? I've been running my whole life. And we all know it's me he wants, so I decided to face him myself."

"He nearly killed you."

"But he didn't. And he won't, not as long as I have my—" I reach up to touch my necklace, and I feel my heart skip. It's not there. "Oh no. My necklace. It's gone!"

I rush to the edge of the cliff, and as I look down over the side, I feel Roman's hands on my shoulders, holding me back.

"It must have fallen in," Roman says.

"No." My eyes fill with tears, and I collapse next to the cauldron. That necklace—my real connection with my mother, the last thing of hers I had—is gone forever, lost due to my own carelessness and recklessness.

And it was also the only thing protecting me from Victor. The only thing that, until now, was keeping me safe.

Twenty-one

Vulnerable. Defenseless. Helpless. These are the words
that run through my head as I lie next to Roman, my head
on his chest. I'm still covered in sweat and soot from the
catacombs, my hand on my collarbone where the necklace used
to be.

"I'll protect you," Roman says.

"That's not it," I say. "It was all I had left of my mom."

"You have your memories."

"I guess that will have to be enough."

Roman runs his hand through my hair. I take a deep breath
and try to relax, but I can't. Not yet. I think we're both in shock
from what just transpired. How close I came to death. How
horrible Roman's encounter with Victor was. He and Alex are
both used to being invincible, and Roman especially—he himself
was like Victor until only recently. For the first time, I'm thinking
that maybe I should leave Lithia for good. Victor is turning out to
be stronger than all of us.

This won't end well. I can feel it in my bones, and it frightens me. And yet there's also this feeling of inevitability—that things will happen a certain way no matter what, and deep down I know I'm powerless to stop it.

I remember what Stan said in the theater: *The difference between tragedy and comedy is all in the timing.* A happy ending versus a tragedy—it's all in the timing. Just like the play, *Romeo and Juliet*. Just like earlier—how close I was to death one minute, and now here I am with Roman. Alive. It could have been so different.

"We need a change of scenery, Katherine." Roman's voice is soft against my cheek.

"What do you mean?"

"I think we should get out of Lithia."

I feel a chill. "You mean leave town? Let Victor win?"

"No, no," he says gently. "I mean temporarily. Just for a little while. A change of pace. Some time to relax."

"What do you have in mind?"

"Europe?" he says. "Asia? The South Pacific?"

"How about Transylvania?"

"Wherever your heart desires, Katherine."

I laugh, despite my gloomy mood. "We both have to be at the theater tomorrow night for the show, remember? How will we have time to fly halfway around the world before then?"

"All right, then. Somewhere close."

"Very close."

"Let's go camping," he says.

"What?" I sit up and look at him, expecting to see a smile. But he's not joking. "You? Camping?"

"Yes, why not?"

I look at him, trying not to laugh again. "I just—well, I never pictured you to be the camping sort. I mean, when I met you, you did live in a castle."

"I'm suppose I may not be *the camping sort*, as you say," Roman says. "But you enjoy it, yes? And if it is relaxing to you, it will be relaxing to me."

"Really? Bugs and rain and sleeping in a tent?"

"I used to work in the mines, you know," he says. "I know how to live out of doors, even if it's been over a hundred years."

"Okay, then. Where?"

"There's a small campsite at the top of Mount Lithia. Normally it's too cold to camp up there this late in the season, but with this warm stretch of weather we've been having, we should be fine tonight."

"Is it safe up there?" I reach up and touch the place where my necklace should be.

"Of course. I'll be there to keep us both safe."

"I'm talking about the volcano, too, not just Victor," I say. "All these earthquakes—and my professor said—"

"Katherine." Roman leans forward and cuts me off with a kiss. "I know that what you saw at Victor's was frightening, but a lot is going on underground, inside the earth, all the time. We just never see it. It doesn't mean the volcano is ready to erupt."

"But Victor—"

"He was trying to frighten you, and he succeeded. You mustn't worry so much."

"I can't help it."

"It would do us both good to get away for an evening. Alex will take care of Lucy. You have nothing to worry about. Let's just have a nice night together and forget about our troubles. There's nothing we can do about Victor tonight anyhow."

He's right. It would be nice to get away. Truly get away. Even if Victor seems to be everywhere, at least if we're outside of town we'll have the illusion of being away. It was a tough day, and I don't think I'll recover from it here in my cottage, or at Roman's house, or anywhere in Lithia, where the specter of Victor hovers everywhere.

"Thank you, Roman."

"For what?" he says.

"For everything. For taking me away tonight. For saving my life this afternoon. I am so lucky to have you."

"Thank *you*, Katherine. It is I who is fortunate."

He gives me another kiss, and then we start getting ready to go. It's already dark, but the slice of moon is rising higher in the sky, and I can tell it's going to be a beautiful night after all.

If only I didn't feel that the worst is yet to come.

The drive to the top of Mount Lithia is one of hairpin turns and switchbacks, and I can't believe I agreed to this at night. Roman is far more confident in his BMW's abilities than I am; I grip the seats as he maneuvers the car up the mountain with startling speed.

"You know, Roman, *I'm* a mortal, even if you're not," I remind him.

"What do you mean, Katherine?"

"Never mind." I can see from the tree line that we're nearly there.

We choose a campsite under a gnarled old tree, bent by wind. Nearby is a barbecue pit and grill, as well as a picnic table; otherwise the campsite is empty—no other tents, no other cars.

I get a small fire going, while Roman parks the car so that the headlights are angled toward our campsite. He removes the tent from the car, and as he puts it down on the ground, I can tell it's brand-new, that it has never been erected before.

And Roman confirms this by the way he's looking at it. Tents must've been a lot less complicated back in his mining days.

"Come on, let me help." The fire is going pretty well, and as we work together to put up the tent, I find that Roman was right—I do feel relaxed. There's something about having a simple task to do that calms the mind, and doing it together is nice, too. We work well as a team. We work in synch with each other, and I can't help admiring the way his muscles look under the snug T-shirt he's wearing.

Once the tent is up, we pull the sleeping bags inside. "It has that new-tent smell," I say.

We grill tofu and vegetables over the fire, and I melt some dark chocolate that we dip fruit into, a sort of camping version of fondue. When we're finished, we clean up everything and secure all the trash into the bear-proof bins.

The stars are out, blanketing the sky in shiny specks of silver, some of them washed out by the light of the sliver of moon.

"How do you like it so far?"

"Camping?" he asks. "I love it. We should do it more often."

"Sounds good to me. For me, this is the best vacation ever." I look over at him, his face so handsome in the firelight. "What about you, Roman? What's your ideal trip?"

"As long as I'm with you, that's where I want to be."

I can't help but smile at this, but I persist. "Come on, you must have a dream trip in mind. You mentioned Europe, Asia—there must be places you want to go."

"I can travel wherever I want very easily," he says. "Time and space don't mean the same thing to us as they do to you. What I have missed all these years is not traveling but feeling at home. Which is how I feel when I'm with you. So that is all I want."

I lean into him and snuggle into the warmth of his body. "I love you," I tell him.

"I love you, too, Katherine," Roman says.

The tree branches creak in the wind, gently, and I feel so far away from all the violence of the past few weeks. It's a feeling I wish I could hold on to forever—a moment I wish I could capture and freeze in time—just Roman and me, with no worries, nothing to stand in our way. Just the two of us. It reminds me of Romeo and Juliet, how the love between them was so complete that they ignored everything else. Of course, it didn't exactly end well for them—but that won't happen to us. Right now, I feel that nothing can come between us, that we will be safe, together, forever.

Twenty-two

I sit up. Something has woken me, but I don't know what. And right now, I don't even know where I am—the darkness is complete, almost suffocating—there's no light at all.

It takes me a moment to remember that Roman is next to me, that we are in a tent on Mount Lithia, that the moon has moved behind the clouds, and that I'm not going to see the light of my alarm clock so I should just stop looking. Roman is still, eyes closed—whatever had woken me must've been my own dream, nothing outside, because he's as quiet as can be.

I lie back down and listen to the wind, watching the sides of the tent pulse in and out like a beating heart. Shadows dance above, and while I try to go back to sleep, I perk up every time I hear a tree creak or branch snap. I know I need to sleep, and I know that Roman, in his meditative half-sleep, would be happy to keep me company if I wanted to talk.

But I'm tired of talking about my fears. I just want to relax. To enjoy the sounds of nature. To let the winds lull me to sleep.

And at some point I do fall back to sleep—only to be awakened by something else, again. This time, I don't lie back down. I sit up, alert, listening. I hear a snap, like a tree branch breaking. I look over at Roman, but his eyes remain closed.

Could it be that I'm hearing things? I feel a rush of air, and all of a sudden, the tent is wide open, the flaps whipping around in the wind. Had we forgotten to close them completely? I crawl over to zip up the flaps. And when I do, I see him.

Despite the blackness of the night, I see Victor hovering above the tent, swaying as if being blown by the wind, yet he is steady enough to hold a sword above him, above our tent. Holding it with both hands, he points it down, over the spot where Roman is resting. Victor's speaking—and somehow I know he's speaking to me, even though he is focused on Roman, and even though I can't understand a word he is saying. His words are jumbled, getting lost in the wind, or maybe it's some strange vampire language that I don't even know.

My breath is coming fast—I open my mouth to ask him what he's doing, and at the same time I turn to wake Roman. But I'm too late—the sword is falling, plunging into the tent, and then I hear a scream—the sound of death and dying, the sound of—

"Katherine!"

Roman is shaking me awake. I realize I'm the one who is screaming.

"Katherine, it's me," he says. "It's all right. You're safe."

Another nightmare. I thought I'd be free of the bad dreams tonight, of all nights. Why here—why now?

I look up at Roman, feel his arms tighten around me, and I exhale. The wind has picked up considerably, and the sides of the tent are flapping like sails. I can see the faint outline of the moon emerging through the clouds, and the shadows of the branches splash human-looking shadows on our tent.

"Better?" Roman asks me.

"It was just a bad dream."

"What about?"

"Victor."

Roman sits up suddenly and leans close to me.

"What exactly did you dream?"

"It's a recurring dream. Same sort of thing, every time."

"What happens?"

"I'm in bed, and Victor is standing above me, about to attack. He is smiling that evil smile of his. And he says something, though I can never quite make it out."

"Try."

"It's just gibberish, really. I don't know."

"Think, Katherine. What does it sound like?"

"Like what language, you mean?" I think about it for a second. "I suppose it sounds most like Latin."

"Try to remember, Katherine."

"What's the big deal? It's just a dream, right?"

"Try."

I close my eyes to conjure back the remnants of the dream, the sounds, as if they are still imprinted on my mind. And, shuddering, I see him again. The pale face. The glowing red eyes. Then he speaks, and I recite it aloud, to Roman, as best I can.

"*Esto perpetua.*"

I open my eyes. Roman's face is eerily serious.

"What does it mean?" I ask.

"It means *May she live forever.*"

"I don't understand."

"It means it wasn't a dream. It means we have to get out of here."

"Leave? Now?"

Roman pushes through the tent flaps and slips outside without making a sound. I start to gather my things in the dark as best I can.

"Hurry," he says.

"I have to pack," I say.

"Leave it. Leave everything."

I climb out of the tent and make my way to the car. Roman is already in the driver's side. He presses the Start button. Nothing happens.

"Damn it, Victor," Roman says.

"Maybe it's just the battery."

"No," he says. "It's Victor."

Roman looks at me in the dim light of the dashboard. I can see worry in his eyes.

"We're going to be okay, right?"

"Of course," he says. "I'm going to work on it for a moment. When you hear me say *start*, push the button."

"Okay."

Roman pops the hood and gets out of the car. My shoulders and neck tense, and I'm scarcely breathing, trying to listen for Victor. I keep looking through the side and back windows for any signs of movement—but, of course, the problem is that you never hear or see Victor until he's right on top of you.

"Start!" Roman calls.

I push the button to start the car, but nothing happens. I hear branches snapping behind us somewhere in the dark, and I look back, seeing nothing but shadows. I can only hope it's the trees blowing in the wind and nothing more.

"Again!" Roman shouts.

I push the button again, and this time the engine comes to life. Roman puts down the hood and gets back in. I lock the doors.

We start down the gravel road. The fog is so thick that Roman has to go slowly, at what feels like a snail's pace.

I hear Roman's name—but how? I don't say it, and there's no one else here. Then, all of a sudden, right in front of the car is Victor, standing there in the middle of the road. I gasp, but instead of stopping, Roman accelerates.

"Roman! What are you doing?"

I hardly know what I'm saying—I know that the only way to stop Victor is to kill him, but at the same time, I find myself completely unprepared for what's about to happen. I brace myself for the impact.

But Victor is smiling, and when we reach the place where he's standing, he's gone. Just like that. As if he were a mirage. A ghost.

I turn around in my seat to look behind us. Victor's not there—I don't see him anywhere. "What just happened?" I ask Roman.

"He's toying with us."

Then there's a massive explosion—I feel it in my bones even before the land in front of us splits open and begins bleeding lava. Roman slams on the brakes. He looks around, then gives me a wry little smile. "It looks as though I should've gotten an all-wheel drive, Katherine. But we'll have to make do."

Then he spins the wheel and turns left, up the impossibly steep old timber road, which probably hasn't been used in years. I can hear the wheels spinning over brush and dips in the earth—for all its glamour, the BMW is barely taking us forward.

"Watch for Victor," Roman says. I press my forehead to the window and survey the cloudy landscape—but it's hard to see anything, with the fog and clouds and smoke, with these blasts of liquid red that we are leaving behind—but not nearly far enough in the distance for my comfort. I can feel the heat from where I am, and some of the lava bursting into the air looks like drippy fireworks. I worry that if it gets any worse—if the lava hurtles any higher into the air—the little flames will hit the trees and burn them down. Once one catches fire, so will the next, and the next, and the next …

I feel my body shaking—I'm trying not to panic, but it's hard not to, knowing that at any moment the ground could open up under us and finish us both off, once and for all. Maybe this had been Victor's plan all along.

Though if I do have to die, at least I'm not alone. At least I'm with Roman.

As if he knows what I'm thinking, Roman reaches over and pats my knee. "We're going to be fine, Katherine. Don't worry."

The BMW makes it up the road, and when we're near the top of the mountain, I look down at the caldera below. There's another road that skirts the back side of the mountain, and we curve around it, away from what's erupting below us. I feel as though I'm living in some sort of bad dream—as though my nightmares are coming to life—as we hit a gravel road, then loop back around to the paved road, finally.

Roman is speeding down the mountain, taking the corners extremely fast, and I want to tell him to slow down but I, too, am in a hurry to be away from Mount Lithia, as far as we can possibly get.

Then I see Lucy, in the middle of the road, looking right at me and waving her arms.

"Roman, stop!"

But it's too late to stop—Roman can only brake and veer off

to the side of the road, and I close my eyes and hold my breath. For a blissful half-second, I'm thinking we got lucky, until I hear a sickening *thump* that almost makes my heart stop.

Then there's silence, stillness.

I open my eyes, daring myself to look at what we've done. "Where is she?"

"Who?" Roman asks. He sounds puzzled, and I look over at him. He's already getting out of the car.

"Lucy, of course," I say as he steps out of the car.

I'm not ready to get out and see her. I wait for Roman to give me some news.

"What do you mean, Katherine?" he's asking. "Lucy isn't here."

I'm so confused I get out of the car and stand next to Roman. We've hit a deer, not Lucy—by the emerging antlers on the head I can tell that this is a young male, lying in the road, injured and unable to stand, but breathing.

Why had I seen Lucy—or thought I had?

But we have other problems to deal with now. I kneel next to the deer and stroke his head; I look into his terrified eyes and try to let him know that he's going to be okay.

He was probably just trying to cross the road to find something else to eat. His eyes are large and black and they watch me closely—we've already hurt him once; how can he know we won't do it again? I can't even imagine what he is thinking right now, what he's feeling—the fear, the shock of humans running into him, then coming so close. "Don't worry," I whisper to him. "We'll take care of you."

Then I straighten up and turn to Roman. "We need to get him to the animal hospital."

"Victor wanted this," Roman says.

"I know. That's why I saw Lucy, isn't it? He made me see her?"

"He wanted us to go off the road," Roman says. I turn to follow his gaze—a steep drop-off, hundreds of feet down. If Roman had veered the wrong way, we'd be at the bottom of that valley right now, in a heap of metal.

"We need to leave, Katherine. Now."

"I know," I say again. I kneel down to the deer again—he must be in shock, and his right hind leg is bloody and twisted. "Help me carry him to the backseat."

I sense him standing above me, pausing. "Katherine—"

"Hurry, Roman."

Roman bends down next to me, and we both take off our jackets to create a clumsy, two-part gurney—but it does the trick. Together we lift the struggling deer, whose hooves ding Roman's car as we carefully fold him into the spacious backseat. I get in after him and continue stroking his head as Roman takes us back to town.

I direct Roman to the Lithia Animal Hospital, where Alex works. I rush in the front door, looking for Alex, calling his name, yelling frantically for help.

An older woman in white emerges from the back. "We hit a deer," I say, "and he's in the car. I don't want to hurt him more by moving him again ourselves."

The woman gets on the phone and says something to someone, and a moment later another woman and a guy emerge from the back with a gurney—basically a stainless steel table on wheels, covered with a blanket. I lead all three of them outside to where Roman is waiting next to the car. They place him gently on the gurney and wheel him in.

The deer is struggling less, weakened from the injury. The three of them disappear in the back. Roman and I just stand there for a moment, and then we decide to sit down. I hear footsteps coming back to the lobby a few moments later and look up. It's Alex, wearing blue scrubs.

I stand up. "How is he?"

"They're getting X-rays right now," Alex says, "and it looks as though his leg is broken, so they'll need to take care of that. Let's hope there aren't any internal injuries."

"Are you going to be back there with him?" I really want to know that Alex will be with him—suddenly it's the most important thing in the world.

He nods. "I will. As soon as the X-rays are done, Alice will come back to tell you what's happening, and to get your approval and your payment information."

"I'll take care of all the charges," Roman says.

I want to reach out and take his hand, but I don't. Because of Alex.

Alex disappears into the back, and about ten minutes later the vet tech, Alice, comes out to the reception desk. "He's got a few cuts and bruises," she says, "but the good news is that there isn't any internal damage. The leg's in pretty bad shape, though—it's broken in two places, and it won't be an easy fix. He's in surgery now, and we'll keep him overnight to see how he does."

I'm so relieved that he'll live that I want to sit down right on the lobby floor. Which, I've just noticed, is covered with drops of blood from the poor deer's broken leg.

She goes over the treatment plan with Roman, and he hands over his credit card. I'm so grateful to him, and confused about why I got so self-conscious about touching him in front of Alex. Alex and I are only friends—and he knows all about me and Roman. I push the thoughts out of my mind. There's enough to think about right now.

Roman and I sit down in the hard plastic chairs in the lobby. I rest my head on his shoulder and say, "Thank you for taking care of him."

"It was me who hit him," Roman says. "It's the very least I can do."

I know that drivers aren't supposed to leave an animal they've hit by the side of the road—but I also know that even when people do the right thing, the animals are often put down. Not everyone would pay a huge vet bill on a deer's behalf. "You're wonderful," I tell Roman.

He smiles at me, then says, "Try to relax. We'll be waiting for a while."

"You don't mind staying?"

"It's probably the safest place for us right now."

With a shudder, I remember seeing Lucy in front of the car, then the feel of us hitting her—only it wasn't her.

"How'd Victor do that?" I ask Roman. "How'd he make me see Lucy when she wasn't there?"

"He's done nothing more than plant the fear in your mind, Katherine. Your own mind does the rest."

I find this hard to believe—the mirage had been so real. Then I sit up, horrified by another thought. "Wait—this doesn't mean Lucy is a vampire, does it? That she could've been attacked?"

"I don't think so," Roman says.

"But she's not with Alex right now. He's been keeping an eye on her."

"I'm sure she's fine, Katherine," Roman says. "Try to rest."

I lay my head back down on his shoulder. I'm far too stressed to sleep, but I close my eyes anyway. I must be more exhausted than I realize because the next thing I know, I'm jerking back upright with a start. Outside the window I can see the faint glow of morning.

"I can't believe I slept," I say. "Any word?"

Roman shakes his head.

I hear footsteps and look up to see Alex.

"How is he?" I ask.

"Surgery went well," Alex says, "but that leg's going to give him a bit of trouble for a while. For now, we've got him sedated and need to watch him through the rest of today."

"I'll be here," I say.

"Katherine, you're exhausted," Roman says. "Allow me."

"I have a better idea—let me keep an eye on him," Alex says. "I actually work here. And you both look like you could use some rest."

"I feel bad leaving," I say.

"There's nothing you can do," Alex says, "and I'll be here all day anyway."

That reminds me. "Alex, where's Lucy?"

"She's in the very capable hands of her new boyfriend, who for some reason she keeps calling Mercutio."

"Are you sure she's safe?"

"Yes, I am," Alex says. "I wouldn't have left her otherwise."

I don't know how he can be so sure—I'm not—but I decide to trust him. "Thanks for looking after her."

Alex nods, then says, "Before you go—there is one issue I need to bring up. About the deer."

"What's that?"

"Well, his leg will heal eventually—but we don't have any sort of rehab available for him to rest as he gets back on his feet. People take their pets home, you know, but wild animals are a different story. They need lots of space, and lots of care. We can't just release this deer back into the wild with an injured leg. And obviously we can't keep him sedated the whole time he recovers."

"What about my land?" I ask. "Can we take him there?"

"That's a good start," Alex says. "But that spot still has a long way to go. At the minimum, we'll need a fence to keep him safe while he recovers."

"I'll build one," I say. "That shouldn't be too hard, since he needs to be in a small space anyway. And we can build a shelter out of one of the smaller foundations so he'll have a place to sleep and rest."

"You'll need to hurry," Alex warns. "We'll need to move him by tomorrow morning."

"That gives me twenty-four hours," I say.

Roman stands. "We'll go pick up fence supplies and tools at the hardware store. I'll see if I can find anyone to come help. We're free until this evening's performance, at least."

As Roman heads out to the car, I pause in the lobby, already taking out my phone to contact Lucy. It's a little early in the day for Lucy, but I consider this an emergency and hope she does, too. At least she probably got a little sleep last night—if she tries to complain, I can mention to her how much less I've slept.

As I text Lucy, I babble to Alex, "And we can build a dog kennel on one of the foundations, and a cat kennel on the other—and we can have fenced areas for all the animals—"

"First things first, Kat. Let's get Walden back on his feet first."

"Walden?"

"That's his name."

"Walden the deer? How'd you come up with that?"

Alex grins. "It was a name I chose for a shelter dog that got adopted, and they changed it to Buster. I just wanted to be sure the name went to a great animal. Even if it's not a pet."

I find myself grinning back. "Works for me." I glance outside the window. "Okay, I better go."

Alex takes my arm, stopping me. "Kat, what happened out there, exactly?" Alex asks.

"Didn't you hear?"

"Hear about what?"

"Mount Lithia."

He shakes his head. "I have no idea what you're talking about. I've been here most of the night, and we haven't heard anything about the mountain."

"We were camping at the top of Mount Lithia," I say. "And parts of the mountain began to erupt."

"Really?" He looks as though he doesn't believe me.

"Didn't anyone in town notice anything? No fire alarms, nothing?"

Alex shakes his head again. "Not that I'm aware of. And we've got the scanner here; it's been asleep. There's nothing coming from the fire or police channels."

"I wonder," I say.

"Wonder what?"

"Well, there was that earthquake at the wedding—and now this. I wonder if Victor has anything to do with it. It's like it's all happening for us and no one else."

"We'll figure it out, Kat. Roman and I haven't given up. You know that."

"I know," I say. "I just worry something will—"

"Stop right there," he says. "Go on—Roman's waiting for you. Like I said, first things first—you have a fence and a barn to build."

Reluctantly I turn to go—and as I do, I get a reply from Lucy. She sounds cranky about the early hour, but writes that she'll be there. With her strong Mercutio, who will also lend a hand.

Twenty-three

It's starting to get dark by the time we're finished—but we've done it.

Roman gathered up six friends from the theater, all stagehands, and they built a small, open structure for Walden to rest and have shelter. We filled it with hay and added a bucket of water. We've put a lot of food in the little barn—plants and leaves, as well as acorns and a variety of fruits—and scattered some about the enclosure to encourage him to get up on his leg when he's ready.

The enclosure is small—about ten feet in diameter—and Alex, Lucy, Mercutio, and a friend of Mercutio's all worked so hard to get the fence raised. It's high enough that Walden can't jump out, and it has extra fencing along the top that turns outward so cougars and other predators can't get in. It's the perfect size for Walden right now. He can't, and shouldn't, go too far on his leg, but it's enough space for him to walk around and, as Alex said, literally get back on his feet.

Alex and a couple of the vet techs are on their way now,

bringing Walden. They've given him another sedative, a mild one, so they'll leave him in his little barn, and Alex will stay up here overnight to keep an eye on him. I've agreed to keep his dogs for now so they don't scare Walden.

We all stand back as Alex, Alice, and two others bring Walden to his shelter. They lay him down in the hay, and he struggles a bit to sit up, then rests again. The veterinarian had said that he'll probably feel as though he can stand up in the next day or so—he's had some pain medication, but it's better not to have too much; if he can't feel pain, he could injure his leg even more without realizing it.

It feels so good to be up here, surrounded by friends, building something to protect Walden—but even better, building the beginning of something that's going to be life changing for so many creatures. When I look around I can tell everyone else feels the magic of it, too—Lucy and Mercutio are arm-in-arm, and Alex is sitting with Walden, petting him gently.

I feel Roman's arm across my shoulders and look up at him. "Thanks so much, Roman. This wouldn't have happened without you."

He smiles. "I think our friend Walden will be very happy here."

"I hope he doesn't have to stay for long. As soon as he's well, he'll be able to head back home." I nod my head in the direction of Mount Lithia.

"I hope that will be soon, too."

As we all get ready to leave, I take one last look at Alex, setting up camp. And then I look back at Mount Lithia, wondering again why the earth shakes and explodes only when Roman and I are around.

—⁓—

Over the next week, it's so quiet that we all relax our never-be-alone rules. Not one of us—Alex or Roman, me or Lucy—has seen or heard a word from Victor. I am tempted to believe it's because he's left town, but I know better.

Roman and Alex are still figuring out how they will take care of Victor, and they won't give me details. They insist that it's good to wait, so that Victor will think we've all gone back to life as normal, that we've let our guards down.

For some reason, I believe that if Victor is going to be killed, I will play a role in it. It's a feeling I don't dare share with Roman. If it frightens me, I know it will terrify him. I don't really want to go back into that house, those caves. I would prefer to live the rest of my life above ground, like anyone else—but there is this feeling, this nagging feeling that we're not near the end, not yet. More like the beginning of the end.

In a way, it's nice to get back to normal life. I have plenty of homework. And plenty of work. And, still hoping to be ready for Cloudline, I run.

But I don't run alone. Roman is always with me, but he's in terrific shape, and I feel as though I'm slowing him down. I know he can hear my labored breathing and that he's patiently keeping pace with me, though I'm sure he wishes he could go all-out. With only one more week to go before Cloudline, I wish I had more miles of training behind me.

I find myself thinking about Erica—if I'd been training properly, I'm sure I'd have seen her on the trails. If I know one thing, it's that she's been training like crazy; it seems that her sole mission in life right now is to beat me in this race. It's weird, being the defending champion—not a role I've played much in life, the person on top, the person everyone wants to knock down. Other than winning a few races back in school, I've always been the one at the bottom, the one coming in last. It's a strange thing to get what you want. I feel as though I have everything I've ever wanted, and even more—but instead of feeling happy, all I can do right now is worry about losing it.

Roman and I are nearing the spot where we'll stop for a break, then turn around—and, as if I've conjured her myself, I see Erica up ahead, jogging in place, taking a drink from a water bottle.

Or, I think I see her. Given the frequency of my "visions" lately, I say to Roman, as casually as I can, "Is that Erica up there?"

"Yes, it is," he says, and when we reach her, we stop and say hello. She nods curtly to us, with the same bitterness on her face as usual. But all of a sudden, there's something familiar about her face—and it only takes a moment to recognize what it is. I'm remembering how I was once as bitter; I was angry at what the world had done to me—taken my mother, left me with a drunk of a father, forcing me to become a runaway. I'd kept it together somehow, thanks to the kindness of strangers—and I was fortunate to have found love and friendship. I wonder if maybe Erica has never been so fortunate. I don't remember any friends here to see her run last year, and she doesn't have a running partner as far as I can tell.

"How's the training going?" I ask, trying to be friendly.

"Excellent," she says, and it's clear that she took my question as a veiled threat. "I'll be ready for you, Pat. Just you wait."

"It's Kat," I tell her—but she's already heading back up the hill, leaving us behind.

And it's probably a good indicator of how the race will turn out that Roman and I are heading back down. "Oh, well," I say.

"Don't worry about her, Katherine," he says. "You just run your own race."

"I suppose I will."

As we take the trails back to town, I resolve not to worry. It's worrying about the outcome that will slow me down, make me nervous and weak. When I run I need to keep my mind clear, my focus only on the path in front of me. Win or lose, I just want to have fun on that trail.

Even now, I know the last mile will be where I win the race or lose it—just like last year, when I overtook Erica with only a few hundred yards to go. She didn't hear me coming until I was past her, and the trail was so steep and she was so winded that she didn't have a chance at catching me.

Now, will it be me who doesn't hear Erica coming up from behind? The last mile of the race is the point at which you are running on fumes, when you tell yourself you've come too far to turn back now, when you ask for a little bit extra from your body, even if that's all you've got left.

The last mile is the most painful mile, and yet it's also the most gratifying. And you can't even get to that last mile without the long journey ahead of it. It's like a rarefied club of those who sacrificed so much just to get in. And it's not even about running, really. It's about pushing yourself in anything, pushing yourself past that point you thought you could not reach, past fear and insecurity, past worrying what others think, past every doubt that ever passed through your mind since you were a child. You push past it all, and you keep pushing on.

—m—

On Monday, with the theater dark, I work with Alex up at the sanctuary. We've set up a temporary campsite; Alex has agreed to come to my cottage in the mornings to shower, to eat, and to see the dogs—even when I'm not there. We take turns walking the dogs during the day, and even Lucy and Mercutio are doing a shift. "Anything they can do as a couple makes them happy," I said to Alex, "so why not take advantage of it? With four dogs and a deer to take care of, we need all the help we can get."

Alex also comes by in the evenings, after his shift at the animal hospital, to prepare food for his dinner and breakfast, and then he's off again. Most of the time, he comes by while I'm working at the theater, but he always leaves me a note, and I find myself looking forward to his tidbits of news—how Walden is, what's new at the animal hospital. Sometimes I get his notes when I get home late at night, and sometimes in the mornings, if I spend the night with Roman. Either way, it seems wrong to look forward to them so much.

Still, as much as I think of Alex, I do know I love Roman. I suppose I'm just feeling jittery about this next stage in my life and worried that Alex and I might drift apart.

On a day like today, though, it feels as though we'll be close forever. We've been working with the architectural firm on plans—a caretaker's cabin, a welcoming and education center, barns for horses, goats, pigs, cows, chickens. Special housing for dogs and cats. A ton of fencing so the animals can roam in their own areas. Replanting of trees so they all have plenty of privacy and shade.

I've signed my will, leaving all the land to Alex. I feel a little disloyal about this, but I know Roman doesn't need this land or care about it the way Alex does. And I need to make sure it's protected from Ed Jacobs and any other developer who might try again to take this property and destroy more of it for homes. While I know Roman wouldn't let that happen, I also know that no one is more passionate about this land than Alex, and I had to choose.

As soon as he finished with my will, Mike started the process of creating a nonprofit for the sanctuary, so we can accept donations. It will be a lot of work, and I'm thinking that now I'll have to add some sort of management study to my degree program to learn how to keep all this going. But it will be worthwhile.

I can see now more than ever how important this will be—not only for rescuing animals who have no place else to go but for the optimism of the whole endeavor. When I'm here, I feel as though there's hope in the world, whether it's seeing people come together to build something or seeing Walden take his first steps after surgery, as he's doing right now. It's a place of hope—and I really need a little of that right about now. The whole world does, for that matter—and we always will.

Alex and I watch as Walden puts more weight tentatively on his right hind leg, then limps a few steps forward.

"He's looking good," I say.

Alex nods. "He'll probably be ready to be on his own in another week or two."

"I'm so glad we could save him."

"Me, too."

We smile at each other, and suddenly, in that moment, I decide to trust him with a plan I've been thinking of but haven't dared say out loud—or even really considered saying out loud. But just now, as I stand here with Alex, it seems as though it's possible—that I might've found a way to conquer Victor after all.

"Alex, can I ask you something?"

"Anything."

"I need your help with something," I say, "but you can't tell anyone. Not even Roman."

"You have a secret you want me to keep from Roman?"

"It's not like that. It's about Victor."

He frowns but says, "Okay. Tell me."

I begin telling him my plan, but before I can even finish the whole scenario, he's shaking his head.

"Kat, this isn't a good idea."

"Why not? You and Roman haven't come up with anything better. You have to admit that, at least."

"Give us a chance."

"You've had your chance. I don't want to wait around for something else to happen. It's been too quiet. That means he's up to something."

"But even so—" He's shaking his head again. "I can't let you do this."

"You have to. You just promised to help me. Besides, my role is minimal. You'll be doing all the work."

"Anything that puts you in harm's way is not what I'd consider minimal."

"It's only for a few minutes. It's nothing."

"What if it doesn't work?"

"It will work," I say. "It has to."

He sighs. "You're right. It has to. It's all we've got."

Twenty-four

I look out the window of my cottage, gazing up at the mountain. I think of the volcano, the recent earthquake—and I don't know what to expect of this land anymore.

But today, all I see is a brilliant blue sky, a scattering of wispy clouds and, beneath them, the tree-studded top of Mount Lithia, as serene as the day I moved here. And it's time to get dressed for Cloudline.

Roman is at his own house getting ready—we're going to meet at the starting line, so I'm wearing a pack so I can carry my cell phone. It'll add some extra weight, but, unlike the last time I ran, there won't be any snow at the top. Lithia's hot summer weather extended well into the fall this year and has kept the snow from sticking, even though temperatures will be in the forties at the top.

Down here, the day will be warm, so I dress in shorts and a tank top; by the time I reach the summit, I won't need another layer. I also don the bright cap that Stacey used to wear—the one I wore to honor her, and the one I hope will bring me luck in today's race.

I walk into town, to the starting line at Manzanita Park. It's early, and the town has not yet awakened. The only people I see are like me, dressed in running gear and headed to the park. We nod at one another, all of us in our own worlds, preparing our minds and bodies for the challenge that awaits.

And it's quite a challenge. Thousands of feet of steep, slanted, twisting nonstop hills. I nearly killed myself last time when I fell off the trail and down the hill, with a tree breaking my descent. It took a ghost to scare me back up and into the race, and I only narrowly won.

I don't feel the same need to win this year, nor to beat Erica. I mostly feel the need to run—to take all that worry and angst I'm feeling and let it out on the trail. It will feel good to be running all-out, and I know that no matter who finishes first, I'll feel so much better by the end.

I'm feeling anxious about my plan for Victor, about keeping it from Roman. I spoke to Alex about it again, and we both know that it's the best option we have. We decided to wait until after the race so we could think about all the angles and make sure we're fully prepared. And I think we will be.

When I reach the starting line I look for Roman, but he's not here yet—or maybe he's already up at the front, where the leaders start. I notice that the crowd this year is larger than before, probably because of the warmer weather and lack of freezing temperatures at the summit.

I look up toward the summit. It looks far more inviting than it did last time, when it was under such a thick cloud we didn't know exactly what the conditions would be like up there, only that they would be very bad. This year, I'm thinking about the opposite— not the freezing cold but the heat of the volcano, and how, given all the recent activity I've witnessed lately, the mountain may not be as dormant as everyone thinks.

I think of the Robert Frost poem, "Fire and Ice"—

Some say the world will end in fire,
Some say in ice.

I hope that in the case of Mount Lithia, it's neither. At least, not for a very long time.

I try to shrug off my anxieties. After all, there's no proof that the volcano is becoming more active—the earthquake wasn't detected, and no one but Roman and me witnessed the bubbling lava that night on the mountain. If Roman hadn't been with me, I'd have guessed it was all in my head.

He's toying with us, Roman had said that night.

Victor. Was he toying with my mind? Or was it him making the earth shake and boil? Is that even possible?

Or is it Gaia, fighting to take back what we've been stealing from her so many years—her trees, her gold, her animals, her water, her air?

"Kat!"

I turn to see Lucy's boyfriend jogging toward me, decked out in running clothes.

"Mercutio!" Thanks to Lucy, I can't help but think of him as Mercutio now—fortunately, he actually enjoys the nickname and is used to answering to Lucy. "You're running?"

He hops from one foot to the other, to stay warmed up. "You bet."

"I didn't even know you were training."

"I like to stay in shape, but you know how Lucy feels about exercise," he says with a laugh. "So, I've been training on my own. Lucy, of course, is sound asleep right now. If she's awake by the time this race is finished, I'll be surprised."

"She's at your place? Alone?"

"Of course," he says. "Where else?"

Lucy and I have been able to avoid sharing with Mercutio all the vampire stuff, for obvious reasons, and we've both spent time alone over the last week or so—but I didn't know Mercutio was running. With Roman coming to join me at the race and Alex up at the sanctuary, I'm concerned. I pull my phone out of my pocket and text Alex. *Will you go check on Lucy? She's alone at Mercutio's.*

No problem, he writes back.

"Something wrong?"

"Oh, nothing," I say, putting my phone away. "Just something I forgot to remind Alex about."

"See you at the top," he says.

"Good luck."

"Right back at you."

I join the runners at the starting line, then look around. Where is Roman? I pull out my phone again and send him a text message. As I wait for a response, I see Erica standing nearby. I smile at her, and she squints back at me.

"Good luck," I say.

"I don't need luck," she says. But even though I can tell she means business today, she smiles in a friendlier way than she ever has.

"Do you have anyone who will be cheering for you?" I ask,

pointing toward the lines of gathering spectators behind the barricades.

She shakes her head. "I'm from California," she says. "A bit of a haul for most people."

"Well, at least there are a lot of locals who come out to watch," I say.

"Mm-hmm."

"How long are you in town?" I ask.

"I usually stay another day or so to rest up before going back," she says, stretching her arms over her head and bending to the side.

"Maybe we could get coffee sometime," I say. She straightens and looks at me, surprised, and I add, "Sometime between when I beat you and when you have to go home, I mean."

She smiles—a real smile, the first time I've ever seen a happy emotion directed toward me. "You wish," she says. Then she adds, "That'd be nice. Loser buys, of course."

"Toss in breakfast," I say, "and you're on."

"Ha," she says. "You better be ready. You have no idea how hungry I'll be after leaving you in the dust."

I laugh, and then I hear the race officials calling us to the starting line. I still have my phone in my hand, and I look down—nothing from Roman. I should've known he wouldn't text back, as technologically challenged as he is—I should've called him instead. But I'd gotten so distracted talking with Erica, and now there's no time.

Cursing myself, I put my phone back in my pack and get ready. The starting gun fires, and I fly onto the trail.

I haven't gone far before I realize that, in my nervousness, I started too fast. I know Erica is behind me, and that's where I should be, too. I usually run better from behind, but at the same time, I'm not ready to slow down just yet—I need to burn off all this extra energy, and if it means losing the race, so be it. Behind me, I can hear Erica breathing heavily as we take our first big turn off of the pavement and onto the steep gravel road.

The hill never gets easy because the hill never gets less steep. The grade hits your legs hard, and you go from a gallop to a crawl in seconds, inching your way up the climb, listening to the sounds of your feet scraping on the gravel. Running up stairs would be faster. But, as with any race, you remind yourself to keep lifting your knees high, to keep your feet under you, to keep climbing.

Running hills requires the ability to look up but not look closely. That is, you need to know where you're headed, but you can't focus on the steep pitch your numb legs have to climb, or they'll rebel and give out on you. You have to trick yourself— keep the body ignorant of what the mind knows is around the next switchback: yet another steep climb.

I'm still on pace with the frontrunners in the lead pack when I hear the first rumble. At first, it doesn't register as an earthquake. I notice others looking up, their rhythm disrupted, but the task at hand is to keep pace, and we move on.

But when the second rumble hits, I feel it in my hips and shoulders, and I can't help but slow down. A few others have slowed, too, but other runners just keep going.

I turn my head to the right and see Erica. I try to make eye contact, but her gaze remains fixed straight ahead.

"Did you feel that?" I ask, between breaths. Erica glances at me but doesn't answer. "The earthquake. Did you feel it?" I ask again.

She shakes her head, and I look behind me at the other women. They, too, are so focused on the race that I could shout *fire!* and they probably wouldn't look up or slow down. Elite runners don't get where they are by being easily distracted.

So what does that say about me?

I've slowed way down, and I'm losing my lead—worse, I'm losing momentum altogether, which is deadly right now if I want to stay in the running. The pack of lead women pull out in front of me. I feel my legs burning, and my eyes wander into the woods, following a strange sound—a clapping noise.

I look to my left, up the hill, and when I see the source, it stops me in my tracks.

Standing tall, towering above the runners on a rock outcropping, is Victor, applauding, that wicked grin of his spreading across his face.

It's been him all along.

Suddenly the earth rises up in front of me, rocking me off my feet. I'm on my knees, and the earth is pliable, moving like waves, and I hear a noise like a train passing by. I try to stand and finally get up, but the only way I can stand is in a surfer's pose, knees bent, arms out for balance. I look behind me and see a dozen or so runners laid out on the dirt.

I smell smoke.

Then I take off at a sprint. I have to stop the leaders from going any farther. They're headed to the top—right into the caldera.

The leaders of the men's race—they're too far along for me to catch them. I don't even know if Roman is among them, but if he is, surely he'll see what's going on and stop them, save them. But if I can't reach the men, at least I can save the women runners.

I come up behind them, yelling for them to stop, to turn around. They glance at me like I'm a madwoman, but I can tell they've been struggling to stay on their feet. They must know— but they aren't listening.

With a burst of energy fueled by fear, I pass them and turn back, waving at them to turn around.

"What is she doing?" I hear one of them say.

"Get out of the way!" another woman shouts at me.

Erica isn't among them, so I turn my back on them and continue up the mountain. In just a few moments, I'm running by Erica's side. By now, smoke is filling the air—why isn't anyone paying attention?

Or, as usual, am I the only one seeing this? Feeling the heat and smelling the smoke?

And where is Roman?

But I don't have the time to find him. I shout Erica's name, and she looks at me, puzzled, but doesn't slow down.

"Erica, we have to turn around!"

"Why?"

"The mountain—it's not safe! Can't you smell the smoke?" I'm coughing now and can't keep up any longer; I have to slow down, let her pass. "Erica!" I call out after her, but either she doesn't hear me or doesn't believe me.

And why should she believe me, if she can't see what I see?

I turn around and hold my arms out as the women I've just left behind come around the switchback.

"Turn! Go back! The mountain isn't safe."

I stretch my arms wide so that anyone who tries to go past me will have to acknowledge me. "Don't go up there! There's a volcano!"

The women slow and stare at me. I hear them murmuring to themselves, and I can feel their doubt and confusion and annoyance, but I persist. "Please, we have to turn back. This mountain is going to erupt any moment. We have to hurry, before it's too late."

Just then the earth heaves, the mountain jerking us all down to its surface, and as we scramble to our feet, I shout, "Come on! Hurry!" and begin to lead them back down the mountain. I hear some of them behind me, but I don't stop and look. I can only save those who want to be saved.

On the way down, we pass other runners still doggedly working their way up the mountain. I'm having a hard time breathing by now, but others have been echoing my cries of danger, and there are enough of us now for the others to realize something's wrong, and everyone begins turning back.

As we meet more runners on their way up, and as more begin to turn around, we slow a bit due to the number of people on the trail. I begin to catch my breath, and I take a quick look behind me, hoping to see Erica among the red, sweaty, worried faces of the runners. But I don't see her anywhere.

Then an explosion stops us all in our tracks, and we turn to see the top of Mount Lithia explode in a burst of red and orange, spraying into the sky like a fire hose of molten earth. *Some say the world will end in fire.*

Lava splashes the sky and begins to drift down, some of it ashy, some of it still fiery, sparking bursts of flames high in the treetops.

We all run almost as if we are one body, all the way back, and it's an excruciatingly slow, smoky haul back down to the starting line. Once there, we see the fire engines heading up the logging roads to put out some of the fires that have started; police and sheriff's vehicles are everywhere.

I scan the crowds for Erica, for Roman—I don't see either one of them. Finally, I see a familiar face—Mercutio, his face covered with soot, his body scratched and burned. But he's okay—he survived.

I keep looking for Erica, but I lose hope quickly; no one who was higher up on the mountain when I turned around has come back.

And I'm convinced I'll see Roman any minute—and then I remember something. Fire—the only thing that can kill a vampire—and Roman had been heading straight into it, into the heart of the volcano.

Have I been wrong all this time? Is it *Roman* Victor has planned to kill all along instead of me—leaving me bereaved instead of Roman?

When you're in love with someone, it doesn't matter. Either way, you lose—whether it's your life or his.

Twenty-five

Lithia's main street is in a state of chaos. Police sirens, the honking of cars trying to get through traffic to escape Lithia, cars and trucks loaded with belongings. People running.

I look up at the smoke rising from the top of Mount Lithia. It's a horrifying sight, and people are wise to flee. I'm again wondering if perhaps my own time has come to leave.

But not yet.

The only chance I have of finding Roman now is my blind hope that he never made it to the race at all. That something held him up. After all, if he'd been there, I'd have seen him.

And Alex. He's in town with Lucy, but I know he'll go to the sanctuary to check on Walden as soon as he can. As far as I can tell, there's no smoke coming from that direction, but it's hard to know for sure. Smoke is drifting from Mount Lithia and settling into the valley, and there's so much of it, it's hard to tell where it's all coming from.

I hurry to Roman's house and pound on his door, but there is no answer. I have a key, but I've left it at my cottage. I put my ear to the door and listen.

"Roman?" I call. "Roman, are you there?"

I hear something, a low moan.

"Roman! Are you okay?"

"Katherine?" Roman's voice is weak and muffled.

"Roman, open the door!" Then I realize he would have already, if he could. "Are you okay? Can you get to the door?"

I listen closely and I hear the bed creak—but no footsteps.

"Roman, stay there. Don't move."

I go around to the side of the house and try each of the windows—all closed. I'm tempted to break one, to get in as quickly as I can, but finally I find a kitchen window that's a few inches open. It's high off the ground, and I have to haul a planter close to the side of the house so that I can stand on it to push the window up and pull myself inside.

I run to the bedroom, where I find Roman in bed. I rush over to him. His eyes are open, but barely. His face is bruised and covered with slashes.

"Roman, what happened?"

"Victor happened," he whispers. He can barely speak.

I lift his shirt, horrified to see that he is covered with blood from cuts that have gone deep—probably from that big knife of Victor's. And the wounds have weakened Roman so much that he can hardly move.

"What do we do?"

Roman is watching me. "I'll be all right."

"Roman, you're bleeding to death."

"It's temporary. I'll heal."

"Are you sure?"

"I promise you, Katherine. I just need time."

"What happened?" But then I realize I already know. "He wanted to stop you from coming to the race. Because he knew you'd be able to save us both."

Roman nods weakly, then smiles. "But you saved yourself, Katherine. Well done."

"I couldn't save everyone." I think of Erica, of all the other runners ahead of us.

I can hear Roman's breathing pick up, and I put an hand on his shoulder. "You need to relax. Get better."

But Roman is trying to sit up. "He's going to destroy Lithia. The volcano will bury everything. Everyone."

"What can you do, in this condition?" I push him back down into the bed, surprised by how weak he truly is. He's in no position to do much of anything.

"We have no choice, Katherine. Victor plans to remove this town from the face of the earth. And we'll all disappear with it if we don't do something now."

"Is this what he's been planning all along?"

"Most likely, yes."

"Cloudline—I should've known," I say. "All those people in one place. All the runners and volunteers and spectators, and the media and the police—"

"Katherine, don't. You could not have stopped this."

"How could I have been so blind? I totally let my guard down."

"What Victor wants, Victor gets. And he's getting more desperate by the day. And I'm beginning to learn why. Word has gotten out, about me and Alex. Others are giving up on blood, including Tyler. Victor is frightened. He wants to wipe the slate clean."

I know what I need to do, but there isn't much time. Roman takes my hand. "I think we must consider leaving Lithia, Katherine. If we do that, he might spare the town. He might spare us."

"Is that what he told you?"

"That is what he implied."

It's tempting, especially right now—though I know Roman doesn't want to leave any more than I do. But right now, I need him to relax, and the only way to do that is to let him believe that I will leave Lithia with him.

"Let me make you some tea," I say.

In the kitchen, I try to think. I look at the open window. While the race had begun early, the hours passed quickly during all the chaos; already I can see shadows in the small backyard.

Then I have an idea—a questionable one, but it's the only thing I can think of right now. If I do this, I'll be able to sneak away for a little while, though I will risk Roman finding out and perhaps never trusting me again. But I don't think Roman will notice—he's still too weak. And it has to be now. As quietly as I can, I slip back out the window.

Ten minutes later, I'm back in the kitchen, where I finish fixing him a cup of tea. When I bring it to him, he asks what took so long, and I tell him the water took a long time to boil.

I sit with him while he drinks his tea. Afterwards, he lies back down, and I caress his forehead until he closes his eyes. I sit there until he falls asleep.

Asleep—a state in which I've never seen Roman.

But it had to be done.

I'd snuck out the window, over to David's house. I know where he keeps a spare key, and I know where he keeps the sleeping pills that he needed after Stacey died. And I know it's the only thing that will keep Roman down long enough for me to do what I plan to do.

Still, I don't have much time—it's getting later by the second, and Roman is never down for long.

I cover Roman with a blanket and head out the door. I don't leave a note. When he awakens and discovers me gone, he'll know exactly where I am. But by then, it will all be over.

Twenty-six

There is no moon tonight, nothing to illuminate the dusky streets as I make my way up the hill to Victor's castle.

I think about what I'm risking and try to tell myself it'll be worth it. The one thing I do know is this: Whatever the outcome of my plan, it's better than the outcome of Victor's plan. We all know that his plan is to kill us all. And if my plan works, we might all be saved—along with the town of Lithia.

And even if my own life comes to an untimely end, I feel ready. The land will be protected, the sanctuary will be born, and animals will be saved. I may not have a chance to marry Roman, but at least I've had the chance to love him. And I'm luckier than most—I've had the chance to love Alex, too.

As I approach Victor's house, I recall my conversation with Alex, not more than an hour earlier.

"It's time," I told him.

"For what?"

"My plan."

"Kat, we haven't thought this through."

"You can see what's going on here, can't you? It's now or never. I'm heading over to Victor's in twenty minutes."

"It's too risky," Alex said. "You shouldn't be going there alone."

"I won't be alone," I told him. "You'll be close behind."

"You're also assuming that I can take on Victor."

"You can. I'll keep him distracted, and you'll just push him over the edge. Simple."

"Simple?" Alex snorted. "Nothing with Victor is simple. Please, Kat. You should listen to Roman and get out of Lithia while you still can."

Not without you, too, I thought but didn't say. Instead, I told him, "I've made up my mind. Victor wants me dead—so, he'll have me dead."

And now, as I look up at his castle, I don't feel as confident as I sounded with Alex.

Victor will have me dead—at least, that's what he will think. He's always one step ahead of us, impossible to trick. But this time, we will be one step ahead of him.

Just as Roman has been playing Romeo onstage, I will now play Juliet in the depths of the earth. I will lure Victor to me, and then I will poison myself so that Victor cannot have me. The poison will infect my blood, making me useless to Victor, and he will be left standing there, standing over my body, making sure I am indeed dead. Perhaps rejoicing. Or perhaps disappointed not to have done it himself. But when he does lean over my lifeless body, at that precise moment, Alex will push Victor into the abyss.

Fire. The one thing that will kill a vampire. Even for a vampire as clever and ruthless as Victor, there is no escaping the bubbling earth inside his cavern.

An hour later, I will awaken. Alex will have carried me home, and Lithia will be saved. The nightmare will be over, finally over.

At least that's the plan.

I know the risks involved. Shakespeare knew them, too, when he hatched the plan for his Juliet.

But Roman is at home, sound asleep—this will all be over before he finds out. Once he learns what I've done, he'll be upset by what I've risked—but he'll forgive me. Because we'll both be safe. We will all be safe.

While I'm putting my life in danger, I would be putting the lives of many, many more in danger by doing nothing. And this knowledge is what propels me forward, forward into the darkness.

As usual, there are no lights on in Victor's home, no signs of life. I stand on the street until I feel a tap on my shoulder. It's Alex.

"This is a bad idea," he says.

"Do you have it?" I ask.

He hands me a small glass vial, small enough to fit in the palm of my hand. The liquid inside is a dark blue.

"If Victor asks, tell him it's cerulean nectar. He'll know you mean business."

"Is that what it is?"

"Of course not. I want you to wake up."

I feel the need to find out exactly what is in the vial, but I don't really want to know. Alex said he could get something that would do the trick—it has to appear as though I am not even breathing—and I trust him. He has access to plenty of drugs at the animal hospital, plenty of potions to put an animal to sleep in a second. And we're all animals, after all.

And right now, as I slip the vial into my pocket and prepare to enter Victor's mansion, I feel more like a non-human animal than a human one. A predator stalking her prey.

"One more thing," Alex says. He reaches into his back pocket and hands me a necklace, silver with a light-green stone, much like the one I lost.

"What's this?"

"I found it in a consignment shop in town."

"Is it like mine? Does it have the same powers?"

"I hope so," he says. "Look, I know it's no replacement for your mom's necklace. But if Victor thinks it's the same one, it might buy you extra time."

"Thank you, Alex." I hug him, but not for too long. It's not *good-bye*, I remind myself, just *thanks*.

"Be safe."

"I will. You, too."

As I turn away, Alex grabs my arm and pulls me to him and gives me a kiss—a long, deep kiss that takes me back to the past, to the redwoods, to our former days and nights together.

"I will always love you," he says.

I will always love you, too, I say back—but not aloud.

Instead I turn and hurry up the steps to the door. It's unlocked, of course. I step inside.

"Victor!" I shout. "I'm here. Come and get me!"

I start toward the stairs heading down. I know exactly where I'm going now. To the basement, through the catacomb of caves and blasting heat and fumes—until I find my way into the great hall. That room with multiple entrances and, at the far end, a deep vat of molten lava.

I shout Victor's name along the way. There's no answer, and a terrible little voice in my head wonders if Victor is even here tonight, if this is all for nothing. But if he's not here now, at this moment, he will be soon enough. It feels as though I'm destined to return to this hellish place. I think I knew the first moment I entered that the only way to kill Victor was down here, in the belly of the beast.

I walk toward the flickering firelight on the far wall. I stop at the edge and look down at the bubbling magma, and I'm surprised to see it so close to the surface, as if it's been rising. It's so close, and for a moment it almost looks inviting—like a swimming pool, ready for me to jump in.

I feel my head go light, and I step back. I reach into my pocket and grab the vial.

I try to imagine Victor's reaction to what I have in store for him. He will think I'm lying; he will doubt that I have the nerve to kill myself, despite my last foolish attempt to outsmart him. But this is exactly why he won't be sure—precisely because I've been so foolish in the past. He knows that I'm pushed to my limit. He will sense my resolve. And I will be wearing my necklace—at least, the necklace he thinks can beat him. He will have to get close to me to be sure—so close that Alex will have the opportunity he needs to do what must be done.

"Hello, my dear."

I turn slowly to face Victor. He stands at the entrance. He doesn't look surprised to see me.

"We have to stop meeting like this."

"That's why I'm here," I say. "To put an end to everything."

He chuckles. "Why so dramatic, dear Katherine?"

"Because it doesn't have to be this way. Because it could've been easy. If you could find it within yourself to change, there would be no more death. You have all the power, and yet you cling to some silly tradition."

"Traditions, as far as vampires are concerned, do not die easily. Humans talk about traditions as if they are forever. Humans have no concept of forever—but we do. We see the earth in eons. Our clocks tick so very slowly. And our traditions are deeply seated. The Greeks and Romans. These are the traditions we speak of."

"What is a tradition, really, but an act that nobody questions anymore? Like eating turkey at Thanksgiving—it's an old tradition, but people keep doing it despite knowing that the turkeys live horrible lives, that those poor birds have nothing to be thankful for." I stop to take a breath. "Since when did repetition take precedence over common sense? If something is wrong, it should end. Every generation has traditions it should keep and traditions it should end for good."

"Perhaps you are right, Katherine. And perhaps I am too weak to question that which I have been given. I'll grant you that. And I'll tell you a secret. To a vampire, the only real enemy is time. Living forever is not a blessing but a curse. A human lifespan is nothing to us—it's a lazy afternoon, which means we are destined to see many people come and go. We will always be left behind. Taking a life gives one a sense of control, a closeness to life, even if it comes at the expense of another life—and so one becomes selfish. To taste life, if only for a few moments, is pleasure. That, my dear, is our darkest secret. That we feed off of humans because we miss *being* human."

He takes a step toward me.

"It's getting hot in here," he says. "As you can see, my little mountain furnace is about to boil over. Soon this cavern will be filled with magma, and then it will bubble up through my home and through the streets. People won't be expecting it so soon, so close to their homes—those who remain here are keeping an eye on the mountain, not on their neighborhoods. Or maybe they are all gone? I hope not. I hope there are people yet to broil."

He takes another step closer. "It's a shame it has to end like this. Your friend Alex is not going to be here to save you."

I stare at Victor as blankly as I can, despite my shock, hoping my face doesn't betray me. Hoping he is just bluffing.

"What are you talking about?" I ask, trying not to let my voice shake. "What does Alex have to do with this?"

"Isn't he the one who is going to sneak up on me?" Victor asks. "He should be here about now, only he has been delayed. I've seen to that. Tragic, really. He'll arrive a few minutes too late. If he arrives at all."

"You're the one who's too late," I say.

"How do you mean, my dear?"

I hold up the vial. "I'm going to beat you to it, Victor. This poison will not only kill me, but it will taint my blood so you can't enjoy it."

Victor smiles. "You're bluffing, my dear."

"Do the words *cerulean nectar* ring a bell?"

Victor jerks his head back as if I've just slapped him. Then he tries to recover. "My, my. I'm surprised Roman would let you do this to yourself."

"Roman doesn't know anything about it. I'm doing this for myself. Sacrificing myself so you will leave Lithia, so you will leave Lithia for good. Wasn't this what you wanted all along?"

Before he can answer I have opened the vial and swallowed the fluid. His eyes glow red and he advances toward me.

"Wait!"

I shake my head. "*Esto perpetua*," I say. "*Esto perpetua*."

I watch him watching me—and what a sight I must be. I hear

the glass vial break near my feet, but I don't remember dropping it. I feel the warmth of the fire on my legs. I begin to lose my balance, and yet I'm looking straight down into a sea of red. I still have the presence of mind to step back, my legs woozy, and turn, away from the cauldron. I drop to my knees, then remember to look up at Victor, who watches me, too stunned to move. And then everything goes black.

Twenty-seven

This is what I've been told. Everything that happened. Everything I did not see.

I was present, but I was not conscious. I was there the whole time but saw nothing. The potion accomplished what it was intended to do—it put me into a deep, sudden sleep.

And in that sleep, around me, a nightmare unfolded.

Victor, as I'd planned, came close to see if I was truly dead—so close Alex could have given him the slightest nudge to push him into the molten lava abyss.

But Alex was not there. Not yet. He had been following close behind me, right on schedule. But just as he was approaching the house, the earth shook, and the entrance to the cavern, the one he was close to passing through, became blocked. I didn't believe Victor at the time—and I had no choice but to follow through with the plan or die by Victor's hand—but I know now that Victor was telling the truth when he said Alex could not make it through to rescue me.

So, as I lay dead—or so Victor thought, since it looked as though I wasn't breathing—Alex, desperate, was forced to find a different route in.

He was only a few seconds late, he said. But in those precious seconds, Roman came in through another entrance.

Roman, who was not supposed to be there. Roman, who had woken early, who had recovered far more quickly than I'd ever imagined, who had dragged his broken body from bed to come looking for me. Roman, who entered the cavern just as Victor was standing over a dead body.

My body.

Roman, who must have assumed right then that Victor had murdered me.

When Alex finally did find a way in, he saw Roman and Victor, hands around each other's necks, on the ground, inches away from my motionless body. Alex said he shouted. He ran. He tried. But he was too late. Before he could reach them, Roman and Victor had rolled over the edge. Into the cauldron, both of them.

Alex said the lava, so close to spilling over, lit up as it consumed them. He had to rush over to drag me out of the way. And only a few moments later, it began to settle. Like boiling water just as the heat is turned off, the bubbling fire began to descend again into its pit. The volcano that Victor promised, the one to consume Lithia, had instead consumed him. And, in doing so, returned to a dormant state. The mountain had returned to its slumber.

Alex carried me home to my cottage. It was there that I first opened my eyes; it was there that Alex told me what happened. The story's ending: Victor's home collapsed into itself moments after Alex carried me out.

I'm not injured physically, but I lie here unable to move, knowing that Roman thought I was dead because of my own daring plan, that he was willing to fight Victor to the death because he thought I was gone and believed there was nothing left for him in the land of the living.

He would be alive now, if only I had done things differently. If only I had left town with him. I hear myself saying it over and over—*if only, if only*—but Alex is quick to argue. He believes that Roman went to the house to take on Victor himself, out of revenge for their earlier fight, and he believes that Roman would have met the same fate either way, only worse—because Victor would still be alive.

And Alex reminds me that if Roman and I had left, the entire town would have been destroyed, covered under hundreds of feet of magma, buried like Pompeii. Countless lives disrupted forever. And how many lives lost?

But when Victor went into the fire, everything changed. Alex said it was strange how I'd come up with that plan—it turned out to be just the thing to end Victor's reign of terror when nothing else could.

But Roman was not supposed to die. That was not part of the plan.

As I lie in bed, the mountain cools. Scientists would later find themselves completely baffled by its sudden dormancy. They would conduct test upon test, but there would be no scientific explanation for what happened.

And, just as quickly as the danger passed, people return. I'm still in bed, not moving, not talking, as residents begin coming home, getting ready for winter. Storefronts putting up holiday decorations. The theater announcing the new season—without Roman. Everything returning to normal, far too quickly for me because nothing is normal, and nothing ever will be again.

But then, life in Lithia never was normal to begin with. And a part of me has always felt that I was destined to live a solitary life.

Like Stan, Roman used to say that acting is all about the timing. Hitting your marks, your entrances, your lines. Every sword fight is timed perfectly so that nobody gets hurt, nobody is in danger. He used to say that he was a successful actor because he had good timing.

Except this time.

But time is not always on your side. Sometimes you just have to accept what happens.

No one knows what happened in Victor's castle—no one but Alex and Lucy and me. People say the house caught fire from one of the bursts of lava spraying over the town during Cloudline. It was a horrible blaze that drew fire trucks from four counties. They poured a river's worth of water on it and protected all nearby homes, but the castle itself was destroyed. The stone walls and turrets and fireplaces all collapsed into a mound of rubble. The fire department found signs of recently cooled lava beneath all the rubble but no bodies. And the town is abuzz about how close it had come to being glazed over by molten lava.

As for Roman, the rumor is that Roman just up and disappeared, like he did before. And because he'd done it before, nobody thinks to go searching for him. Few people knew we were a couple, that we were engaged, so I get no questions, and I let them believe what they want. To them, he's just another temperamental actor, taking off to find himself, heading to Hollywood. They say he'll be back, just like before. That's the part I wish were true.

Twenty-eight

I have spent far too much of my time in Lithia in the cemetery, and I suppose by now I always will. Visiting my mom, and Stacey, and now Roman.

I know I should join the world of the living. I know I should emerge from my bed and demonstrate to everyone that I'm okay, that I'm strong, that I'll get through this.

But lying in bed, head pulled under the sheets, I don't feel so strong. In the darkness I can still imagine that he is with me, as he was that night we shared in the tent. I can still hear the wind against the bedsheets.

I know I must emerge now from the safety of these sheets. I know I must face the world, if for no other reason than to stop everyone from worrying over me.

Alex is spending too much time looking after me, when he should be at the sanctuary. Lucy is missing school and time with Mercutio to try to comfort me, when nothing works anyway. She told Mercutio what most people are saying, that Roman took off and left me, and even he comes over one day with a book of Shakespeare jokes and a box of vegan doughnuts to try to cheer me. David and Kendra return, so happy in their new marriage that I can't bear to bring them down. Despite everything, I have people who love me. People in the world of the living.

And so I get up. I get dressed. I leave the cottage to face the world.

But within minutes I've returned to the cemetery, to the world of the dead. And I tell myself that, still, this is progress. I'm out of my house. I'm breathing in fresh air, surprisingly clear of smoke so soon after the volcano.

Right now, the cemetery is the only place I want to be. I go alone, as I always do. I stand by Roman's grave. Of course, no one even knows he perished—the grave I visit is the first one, from long ago, from the first time he died and became who he was when I met him. I look at his old, weathered headstone—the grave that has never held a body, the grave for a miner lost in the earth. And I suppose this is more true than ever before.

Roman
B. 1836 D. 1861

"I'm sorry, Roman. I never would have done this if I'd known it would end this way."

I talk to him the way I talk to my mom, as if he can hear me. And, as with her, I feel that he's listening.

"I really wanted to be married to you. I was looking forward to our life together. I wish I'd confided in you about the plan. I hope you'll forgive me."

I kneel down by his grave, touching the cool, century-old headstone. I've brought a photo of us from David and Kendra's wedding. I hold it out, as if he can see it. "This is what I imagine our wedding would've been like. And in a way, it feels like it already happened. Because I think we were already married to each other in so many ways."

I stay there for a bit longer, listening closely to the silence, hoping that I might hear his voice one last time. Finally I stand up. "I love you, Roman," I say. I lean over and kiss the headstone. My lips feel warmth from the stone even though it sits in the shade.

"I miss you. I will always miss you."

And then I turn and walk away. But not forever. I have two more graves to visit here today, and I will always be back. This is where the people I love the most live now.

But I need to remember that there are other people I love—people who are alive and well and worried about me. People who need me as much as I need them. So I try to return to life as usual.

I take my things out of Roman's house and say good-bye to it. The landlord is going to rent it out again, to some other actor, probably. And when I return to my cottage, I find Alex there, with a couple of surprises. Small, furry surprises.

There are two kittens and an older cat snuggled together on my bed, the little ones curled up under the big one as if she's one big blanket. "They were dropped off at the shelter," Alex tells me, "by someone who found them in a box by the road."

Horrible, what people to do animals. Finally, something replaces the grief that's been overpowering me—anger, disbelief.

"They normally would go into a holding room for a week or two," Alex says, "but I took them straight to the animal hospital. The kittens are two months old, and the older one is their mom. They've all been fixed and vaccinated, and they're yours. If you want them."

"How could I not?" I go to the bed and stroke the head of the mama cat. She looks up at me with sleepy eyes, then stretches her legs around her kittens, pulling them closer. Then she closes her eyes. The kittens don't even move.

"They're beautiful," I murmur. The mom is black with a white chin and belly, and white paws. The kittens have black and white patterns that make them look like tiny cows. "They're perfect," I say to Alex. "Thank you."

I name the mama cat after my mom. The two kittens, a boy and a girl, I call Stacey and Roman. I know some people might find that ghoulish or even offensive, but to me it's the highest honor I could give, both to the kittens and to the people I've lost. Alex agrees, and even David understands, especially when he sees how much I love the little kitten named Stacey. And he is a fellow vegan, after all; he places non-human animals right up there with the human ones. "She even reminds me of her," he says once, when he sees how spunky the little kitten is.

Up at the Lithia Animal Sanctuary, things are moving right along. Construction has begun on the cat and dog kennels, and the sounds of hammering and sawing echo down the valley. Volunteers are putting up fences so the animals have plenty of outdoor space as well as their kennels and playrooms inside. Once this is done, we'll begin raising money for the second phase, the sanctuaries for farm animals.

Alex is working on getting his certification as a vet tech, and his cabin should be finished even before the kennel buildings are done. Despite everything, there are good things happening in Lithia—at last.

Walden has recovered well, and the time finally comes to release him back into the woods. I know it's time to let him go, but I don't feel quite ready—it's almost as if he's the last connection I have to Roman: our night together, Roman's generosity in paying for Walden's care and getting the fence started.

But we can't hold on forever. Alex opens the gate to the fence, and we stand back. We've made sure to give Walden his space; Alex has only approached him a few times, with Alice's help, to get a look at his leg to make sure it's healing well—we didn't want Walden to become too socialized. I was tempted to keep him here all winter, where he'd have plenty of food and where he'd be safe from cougars, but Alex reminded me that we have no business penning in a wild animal, not now that he's well. And I had to admit that Alex is right. And he'll head into winter as fit and healthy as any deer in the forest.

We watch and wait as Walden looks around for any leftover fruit or nuts in his enclosure. Finding it bare, he looks up to see the fence wide open. He takes a few tentative steps forward—solid, healthy steps—then continues through. As Alex and I turn to watch him disappear into the woods, I feel the warmth of Alex's hand in mine.

In the next couple of weeks, I try to get my life in order. It feels good to be keeping busy so I don't have to think so much about the past—so I can focus on the future. *Romeo and Juliet* has ended, and I've decided to end my work at the theater. It's too painful to be there; I still expect to see Roman on the stage, and I may never get used to the fact that he'll never be there again. But maybe Lucy will be on the stage one day—and for that I would return. I hope to convince her, once she graduates, to stay on in Lithia instead of going to New York or LA.

Meanwhile, I have missed so many classes that I have to take incompletes and start over. This time, I register as a full-time student. And I sign up for a class in nonprofit management.

I haven't gone for a run since Cloudline—that, too, has been too painful to think about. But I know it's too big a part of me to ignore forever. So I lace up my worn-out running shoes and head up into the hills. It's early, quiet—just me and the sounds of my feet on dirt and gravel. Then the sound of my breath as I climb the trail and start to wind my way up the steep hills. Toward the sanctuary.

When I get to a clearing, I stop and look out over Lithia. I hear a noise and I swing around, heart stopping mid-beat. But it is only a deer. She eyes me tentatively, then continues to nibble on the leaves of small tree. I feel as though she's reminding me that I will never be alone. And that I have nothing more in these woods to fear. All that's left here are those who belong.

When I get to the sanctuary, I greet Alex, who's been spending most of his time up here now that his cabin is almost finished. He says, "I'm glad you're here. Sit down. I have something for you."

He goes over to his tent and comes back as I sit on a large boulder. He reaches for my hand, and when I give it to him, he places my mother's serpentine necklace in my palm.

"Is this—is this real?"

He nods. "It's yours. I found it at Victor's. But you were in such a state I knew I couldn't give it to you before now. I wanted to wait until you were ready."

"I've never been more ready."

He takes it from me again. "Let me put it on for you."

I feel better the moment I feel its weight on my neck. I won't need it for protection any longer, just for the memories.

Alex kisses the top of my head before sitting down next to me, one of the many sweet gestures he's extended since that awful night. While I know I still love him, he seems to know that I need time to recover from losing Roman—and yet it feels as though wherever we're headed, it'll be a good place to be once time heals and we eventually get there.

We sit in silence, listening to the sounds of the woods around us—the birds, the wind in the trees, the crunch of branches as unseen deer forage in the brush. Alex's dogs are running around in one of the fenced enclosures, barking playfully every once in a while. We sit and enjoy the sounds as if we're listening to a symphony. The optimistic melody of the birds. The relaxing rhythm of the wind through the leaves. The sounds of nature at one with itself, again. The sounds of peace.

And right now, it feels as though the music will play forever.

About the Author

Blair Richmond is the pen name of a writer who lives
in the Pacific Northwest. *The Last Mile* is the third
book in the Lithia Trilogy. To learn more,
visit http://blairrichmond.blogspot.com.

Ashland
Creek
Press

Ashland Creek Press is an independent publisher of books with a world view. From travel narratives to eco-literature, our mission is to publish a range of books that foster an appreciation for worlds outside our own, for nature and the animal kingdom, and for the ways in which we all connect. To keep up-to-date on new and forthcoming books, subscribe to our free newsletter at www.AshlandCreekPress.com.